PEACOCK DANCER

AND OTHER WORKS

CATHERINE MINTZ

Published by Copper Publishing 2010

www.copper-publishing.com

978-0-9826590-1-4

Table of Contents

Peacock Dancer

I rake a metal-shod foot on the floor with a menacing rasp, flex my arms and step into the courtyard as a riff of rain splatters its gray stone and makes the torches gutter. Alone, I move to the constant peal of the water chimes, testing the linkages. In the puddles, my reflection follows, foot-to-foot, hand to hand. That twin and I are as one, perfectly mirrored.

Tomorrow I will dance my last dance. Sumalee is ten years younger than I but we are twins. She was created and raised to take my place. I should be proud they think so highly of me, but my art is my own, not something written in my genes. I lower my arms and hear the hiss of raw power meeting water. Vowing I will not spoil this moment with anger, I vibrate my metal-decked arms until they sing true.

I invoke phantom drums. Five beats I wait, turn my head left, right, left, and wait again. Right, left, right. The imaginary flute enters and I light my suit, spread my peacock tail. The courtyard flames with purples, greens, and blues. If it were not for the insistent rhythm in my head, I would be shocked still. Palm leaves drip gems and stone carvings glisten.

With a tremolo like nothing that has ever been played, I am the peacock, dancing the universe into being. Raindrops become stars. Splashing water spins into galaxies. My feet rasp the measured pace of time. I dance until there is no beat but the drumming of my heart and the suit's power is exhausted. Fading, I sink onto the paving in the rain, and weep, not for sadness, but because it was so beautiful.

The clop of wet hands applauding spoils the moment. I shiver with disgust. I know who it is: Administrator Pravat, drawn here by the light. My face as impassive as I can make it, I bow to my unwanted audience and walk off, into the rain, into the darkness, stripping off my suit as I go. I am tempted to let the pieces fall where they may but I resist. I will give them nothing to complain about.

Why should I do what they want? I ask myself. I will not dance tomorrow or ever again: a small revolt against the iron rule of the Benevolent Autocracy. Leaving my suit in my room, I don coarse clothes, slip through the doors, and start down the road I climbed so many years ago. I came crying and I leave crying.

The road is rough-paved, with stones on either side. I lurch from marker to marker, near blind with rain and tears. My heart aches, not because I must go—I have always known this would come—but because my final dance for myself has been spoiled. I will never wear my suit—their suit—again. I wanted to dance one last time for no one but myself.

Administrator Pravat took that away from me. I loathe his red hair, his beak of a nose, and his thick hands. Most of all I hate his false name, chosen to be easy to pronounce, as if we were tongue-tied fools. He may rule us but he has no business among us. Why can't he leave us alone!

His people find mine quaint, ethnic, and amusing. For them the great market of the port is a tourist paradise. For us, it is an economic necessity. We need hard cash for new crops, medicines, and the communication feed that tells us market prices. In the Autocracy, everything must be profitable.

I wish he had never seen me. Month after month, he has come and asked if it was time for me to retire, was my replacement ready, when would it be. I must not wail aloud. Someone might think I was possessed, phi pob. Such people are driven up into the hills, to live among their own kind. As a child, I wondered what it was like. As an adult—sixteen standard years—I don't want to know.

Lowering my battered hat, biting a fold of my shirt to keep

myself silent, I walk on through stinging rain. I smell the farm long before I can see it. My family fattens pigs and there are overripe bananas in the trough in the hog house. My nose twitches at the stench but I knock on the door.

"You are early," my father says, lifting a light to see me better.

"Early is better than late or not at all," I reply. It's like a password back into my childhood; one I wish I did not have to give.

He smiles his thin, hard smile. Father did very well by selling me as a dancer. They came and auditioned me, as they do most of the girls, but for me he got a fee, in gold, that doubled the size of the holding.

His eyes soften a little, probably with the memory of how well he did then. "Tonight, drink tea and go to bed. I will expect you up with the others in the morning."

"Yes," I say, head bowed, demure. It would never occur to him that I have been taught to behave one way and think another.

"She has soft hands," says one of my stepmothers from her place in darkness. Light takes power. Farmers do not waste power.

"They will harden," my father replies.

"She is not ugly," she answers. "We might do better if—"

Then I am out of hearing. The kitchen is bright and hot, although most of the work is done. I remember the cook, although not well. A stout, brisk woman who cooks for twenty or more people, Rajini seldom has a moment to herself. She keeps congee on the simmer all night long and water near the boil for the emergencies, big and small, of so large a holding. The methane-powered steamer that prepares garbage for pig food stands gleaming, ready for the morning.

She asks, "Have you eaten?"

"No," I say.

Without a word, she cracks an egg into a bowl, ladles in

simmering congee. Then she adds shredded roast pork, green onion, and a dot of chili paste. Finally, she places the bowl on the rough kitchen table, puts down a spoon, and indicates a stool. I draw up the seat and sit in my wet clothes, which have begun to steam. I try to fill the hollow in me with food. It is not hunger that makes me empty, but I feel better when I am done.

"You're wet and dirty," says the cook, rinsing my bowl. "It's too late for a bath or laundry. There's sacking piled there. Sleep near the hearth and feed the fire. That charcoal should last past dawn. I'll want a hot, bright blaze for the morning tea."

"Yes," I say, and Rajini is gone. No telling where. I can hardly complain at being pressed into service, since she fed me better than my father thought necessary: rough but not unkind. I wonder what she dreams or if she dreams at all. Out in the yard, a peacock screams, and fusses back to sleep. My eyes tear and I remember.

Mother wasn't really beautiful, of course, just beautiful as all mothers are to their children. She was uncommonly graceful and when the day's chores were done, she would show me this or that dance step, or sit, laughing, my baby brother in her arms, while I made up my own. I had been some time at the Hall before I understood how carefully she trained me.

I lost her and my brother died during one of the periods when the Autocracy suspended trade and no medicines were available for perpetually cash-poor farmers. My father had brought home chickens the week before, a strain that would reach market size faster. They were gorgeous.

My brother, intrigued by the cocks' red wings and blue-black tail feathers, chased one of them through the kitchen and into the house. Father had to let him keep that one as a pet to get him to leave the rest alone. When it grew ill and then died, my father didn't think much of it. Chickens pick up human diseases easily.

Then my brother fell sick. My mother nursed him constantly until she caught influenza also. They both died on the same night. Two weeks later, I was tested and on my way to the Hall, arm stinging with a vaccination. My father's messages, never very long, grew infrequent, and then ceased. When I heard he had married again, two sisters, I thought I would never return home.

Yet here I am. The compound is quiet, except for an occasional grunt from the hogs and a sleepy cackle from the hens, still penned near the house, theft being rated a greater risk than disease. A gust of damp air carries the ammonic reek of chicken manure to me, and I cough.

I feed charcoal to the fire, bit by bit, tucking the pieces into the coals as my mother once did, while the rain dies away. When I look out, there is moon-glow behind the clouds. My clothes are dry. I take a tiffin box, fill one layer with cold rice and tuck pickled chilies in the center. There's nothing handy to put in the other, so I add more rice. It will be a long walk.

I am not unknown in the city. It seems likely I can do better for myself than my stepmothers might. Tiffin box in hand, I slip out the door and begin the walk to Chiang Dao, Star City, the place of spirits. Ghost-faced foreigners call it Mongkut Starport.

The lower valley is spangled with fires: farmers out harvesting for market, delayed by the rain. I can smell smoke, bananas, and papaya. The wind is rising and the clouds drifting away. I am beyond my family's land when I pause, look back, and see what I had taken for the rising moon is the glow from the hall on the mountain. The place is ablaze with lights.

For an instant, I think stars in the sky are moving. Helies are seldom used at night but there are a least a dozen in the sky. I look toward the city. There is nothing on the road before me. There is nothing on the road back. I am alone and highly visible. Without thinking, I crouch behind a stone, listening.

The light hits me like a slap. I stand, ashamed to be caught huddled in the dark. "JAIDEE!" My name, roaring out of the sky like thunder.

"Yes," I say, and feel foolish. My voice is so soft.

"WHAT ARE YOU DOING?"

"I'm going to the city." I might as well say it. The road ends at the city. There's nothing beyond it but the paved plain where shuttles land and leave, hammering their way to low orbit.

"DON'T MOVE. WE'RE COMING DOWN."

With a blast of hot air, the heli settles to the road. Guards pour out of it like water from a broken jug. They have me by the arms before I can react, lift and carry me to the heli before I think to resist. The voice was that of Administrator Pravat. "You've put me to a lot of trouble," he says, "Why?"

"I went home."

He waits.

I wait, too.

"You didn't stay," he says.

"No."

"Sit there."

Like a dog, I sit in the indicated seat. The soldiers strap in. The heli lurches into the air, and turns east, toward the city.

"Where are we going?" I ask, startled. The worst I had expected would be that he would expect me to dance and accept defeat publicly. He ignores me, giving me plenty of time to struggle with my unhappy stomach as I take my first flight. I grip my tiffin box and wish I hadn't brought it.

The best thing I can say about it is the heli takes minutes to cover a distance I would take a day to walk. The worst is that I have utterly no dignity left when I stagger off. Despite the odor, the Administrator pays no attention. The soldiers are stoic.

I trip getting out and rice, red with chilies, is strewn everywhere. Someone stumbles on the mess and the dented box rolls off, clanging. I squat without thinking, trying to gather it together. The solders laugh and walk on. I sit back on my heels, carefully expressionless. I hadn't realized how much I wanted that taste of home until I saw it ground underfoot.

"Come," says the Administrator. "Come with me. There's nothing to be done about it." I look up. He offers me a hand, not flinching when I give him mine, which is filthy. "We go this way," he says when I start after the soldiers. I release his hand, but follow him.

The building is a maze crowded with shops. I smell fried fish, perfume, mangos, and something indefinable, perhaps from off world. Punctuated by the clangor of metal-smiths, the din is staggering. A child wails and no one bothers to look. Everyone moves as if they were alone.

"This way," says the Administrator. "You can look around later." Then he really looks at me and adds, "If you want. It's not such a big place, once you know your way around." I follow him like a homeless puppy, through one door and then another. The smells and noise fade away. My lungs almost hurt with the cold, clean air and I can hear our footsteps.

"Now," says Administrator Pravat, once we are seated in an office. "I had thought to talk to you after your final dance, but since you left early, it has taken me some effort to locate you." He pauses. He expects me to say I am sorry. I am not. He blinks, and cuts whatever he was going to say short. "I have something special in mind for you. Come."

I stay sitting just long enough to make him think I might not come, then rise like the dancer I am. We go through another door. I can hear the thud of a drum, the plink-plink of someone tuning, voices wailing and howling in warm-up. Administrator Pravat flinches and walks faster. I have a hard time keeping up gracefully. "Where are we going?" I say.

He raps on a door and opens it without waiting. "Here," he says, and ushers me ahead of him. I start back and he laughs. The creature is taller than a tall man, and stands on four legs, with two large arms and two small ones. The hands have three digits. The head is grotesque, covered with bosses and spikes. Administrator Pravat slaps a switch and the projection fades, revealing a suit much like the one I dance the peacock dance in. "Put it on," he says.

It is not so much a matter of putting it on as fitting myself into it. I check the suit out thoroughly, locating all the contacts, the power packs, testing the joints and linkages. Finally I stand there caparisoned in metal and projectors. "Turn it on," says Administrator Pravat, and I do. He steps back, cautious. I move slowly, testing the strange form I wear. "Can you make it dance?" he asks.

"Yes," I say, and my four arms rise to an unheard drumbeat then fall as I make my first step. Without hurry, I begin improvising, testing. I had thought I would never again feel the smooth pivoting of powerful machinery at my command. The suit, mirrored in the safety screen, has a strange beauty.

I open my arms, and four cream-dappled arms open. I nod and a helmeted head nods. When I step, four tawny-stippled legs tap on the floor. I step again: there is sound. I turn, listening. The body made of light watches itself with great gold eyes. I am slow but not awkward. I will be able to dance in this suit.

I began, something simple, listening to the staccato of my phantom feet on the floor. I clap two pairs of not quite hands, and they sound. I imagine a descant, like wind running over grass, through cane, through leaves. I crouch: this is a hunter's body. I spring, recover, crouch again, creep forward, slowly and silently.

Behind the safety screen, Administrator Pravat watches. "Stop," he says, finally. "Good. Very good. Will you do it?"

"I don't know what you are asking."

"They," he points to the suit, "don't speak, although they do make noises. We think their language is gestures, but it might be something else. We need to find out. This may be the best way."

Securing the suit, I work myself out of it. I know I don't want to say no. The feel of the machinery around me is too welcome for that. There's a roughness in the way the suit moves, something to work around. "I'll need to know more, to practice with this, before I decide."

I am afraid to say yes. I know people who have dreamed of going off world: my father once did. Now he spends his days in the orchards, packing fruit, fattening pigs and raising chickens. I need time to think. "Will it be dangerous?" I ask, and then, "Where is it? This place?"

Administrator Pravat doesn't bother to reply, just gestures me to follow. My hair lashes my face as we walk through a curtain of wind. Beyond the archway I see sunlight and sniff a fragrance I cannot place. Administrator Pravat motions that I should go first. I hesitate. He smiles. I stagger into the sunshine. Behind me, he says, "It looks like this."

A fountain, its jets leaping to the music of wind chimes, forms a backdrop for a dancing court, much like the one at the Hall. After that, the resemblance to anything I have ever seen ends. I take a deep, wondering breath. It is a world of beiges, browns, tans, all dappled with light and striped with restless shadows.

White flowers wider than my hand crowd the basin and spill into the water. Feeling off-balance, I walk forward and touch the silky cold surface. It is mountain water, nearly as cold as ice, for all the stone under my feet is hot.

"You'll notice the gravity is lighter and the sun more yellow," says Administrator Pravat. "You will need practice to move well. There are about a hundred days until the ship leaves. Maybe a hundred and fifty. If you don't want to go, perhaps you can teach—"

I have no idea what my expression is, but he grins, suddenly almost likeable. "Your room is over there. There are recordings, notes, and communications. After you go through those, if you need anything, ask. I'll see you tomorrow." With that, he walks through the curtain of wind.

In my coarse clothes, filthy with the dirt of this world, I sit on the edge of the fountain and look into the water. Pisciforms swim through the depths, indifferent to anything beyond their watery universe. The surface ripples with reflections: the exotic blossoms, the hologram of the foreign sun, and my own earnest face, framed by my farmer's hat.

Behind me stands my phantom second self, four-armed, four-legged and so real that I look around, startled. There's nothing there, of course. I can feel that body. It can run, fast and quiet. It can wait, without moving, watching the sun crawl across the sky. It hungers. It hates. It loves, and dreams, and dances.

I sniff my hands. They smell of rice, chilies, and earth. The other world won't smell like that. The food will be odd. The people will not be my people. It's frightening, thinking of all the differences. But I am a dancer. I rise, needing to don the suit that I will make my second self.

Like hail on paving a hundred metal feet step in unison. I make it through the entire set without error and stand, panting, hoping not to be noticed. Not to be noticed is the greatest praise here. I must move at the will of the negotiator, who will sit safe in a cubical, testing the reactions of the people we have come among, uninvited. All of the danger will be mine but little of the glory. I am a tool and a poor one, at that.

My suit and I cannot move as they move. If I flex a limb, the motion is not and never can be right. That you can never do something more than acceptably is demoralizing. Still, muscles quivering, I stand, ready. As the suits draw down their power supplies, they become harder to move, harder to hold in position. We've done well and are too tired to do better. Some days Sensei is merciful.

Not today.

"You are tired," she says in her meticulous Omlingual, "but you will have to work when you are tired and when you are sick. You have to learn how to keep going and to do everything precisely. There is no room for error. Ever."

There is a splash of metal on paving: a suit, unlinked.

Sensei's face does not change. It never changes when someone resigns. She gives us a moment while the name passes among us like wind through dry grass. Lisabet was a good dancer. Her resignation shakes us all. Trained to wring one more dance, one more sequence, one more step from unwilling bodies, we may not be all they want but we are the best there is.

"Our future—and theirs—depends on your conveying meaning correctly. Again," says Sensei.

Minus one, once more our metal-shod feet step in unison.

I blush whenever I remember how graciously I accepted Administrator Pravat's invitation, how stunned I was when he said, "Good. Let's join the rest." He opened a door and there they were, fifty-three girls—women—all competing for positions.

I was young, and afraid to tell anyone I was frightened of failure. Death didn't seem nearly as scary, but that was before my first—and only—space flight, one long fall into darkness. Home is a long way away. There are only seventeen of us now. Some nights I dream of unlinking my suit and wake up crying, not knowing if I am happy or sad.

Class finishes. The others scatter singly to their rooms or jointly out into the city. At time-lived twenty, real-time thirty-one, I am younger than the rest, which makes me an outsider. Alone, I habitually go into the deserted garden and perform the dances I learned as a child—the lotus, the caterpillar, and the butterfly. If I am especially sad or happy, I dance the peacock.

I don't have my suit, of course, but children don't dance in suits. They wear bustles and wings of braided palm leaves that they make themselves. There are no palms here, but the covered basket of garden refuse at the gate always has plenty of leaves and stems. I enjoy the handiwork, like dancing with my fingers.

By now, I am nimble in my improvising. This afternoon, there are flowers heaped beside the trash, ripped from the beds and replaced. White, cream, and gold, their saffron pollen dusts my hands are I work them into patterns, making them beautiful one last time. I sniff, my hands smell of dust and something aromatic that makes my nose itch. I sneeze.

Listening to the wind chimes, I fasten my bustle and slide my wings on. Focused by tiny holes in my bustle and wings minute suns spangle the pavement at my feet. In a shower of pollen, I begin the peacock dance, turning and turning, then stop and begin again. Frowning, I clap time for myself, a little slower than usual, a rhythm for late afternoon. I can leap high in the light gravity: it changes the pace of the dance.

My foot slides on the paving and I am the peacock. My shadow follows, foot-to-foot, hand to hand. Suns swirl about me. My wings loose time winds, scattering saffron dust over the world I dance alive. The universe spins as I dance. Suns spill into the heart of the galaxy. Heavier, heavier, it sinks into darkness, then explodes into new glory.

I finish—wings flung wide, tail spread—and stand quivering as I return to time and place. Time and place and an odd tapping: I turn around. Someone has come into the garden wearing a suit. I blush furiously, drop my improvised costume, crush it in my arms, and bolt for the gate. With a smooth tap-tapping of feet on paving the suit glides to block it.

Angry, I hold my armload high in front of me. I want out, even if I am undignified, because I'm going to cry. Which is why I am face to face, tears dripping off my chin, before I realize my audience is not wearing a suit. I gasp and drop the trash that was my costume.

The dapples and stipples are marks of rank, affiliation, and gender. The alien is very important. It would—I shiver—have to be important to be here, in our compound, unescorted. I see gold and garnets on its carapace. It reaches out—

Something touches my face, the velvety palp they use for fine touching. They don't speak, although frightened or hurt they can produce a shrill whistle. I back away. It rattles its feet on the paving, gathers up my armload and offers it to me with its lesser arms.

"Please," I say. "It's—not important."

It thrums its feet on the paving, demanding more. We know a few simple gestures and that is what this one means: do it again.

It was embarrassing to be caught out, frightening to find what my audience is, but—to perform. I bite my lip and swallow hard. I can't refuse. Everything I—everything we—everything everyone—has done up to now was to win this opportunity. At least I can't make a mistake, offend doing my own dance. Can I? It saw—

I take the offered armload, fearing the costume is too crushed to wear. My fingers fumble as I pull it into shape. I replace flowers almost at random until my legs can hold me. I put my costume on and close my eyes a moment to center myself. I slide one foot on the paving and I become—something new.

With a staccato rattle, my audience begins to dance, too. Suns swirl about us as our feet scatter saffron dust over the world we dance alive, into darkness, then into new glory while the wind chimes peal.

Greenwife

T he crow that had been following the only moving thing in the white landscape cawed once and flew on, straight toward the horizon. I turned the wheel, felt my car slither until its wheels bounced back into the furrows ploughed by earlier travelers. Three miles to Three Corners. I could stop and think about whether to go on when I got there. Right now the road required all my attention.

I was already past the van left nose-down in the ditch when the driver's door popped open. A bundled figure scrambled into the road and waved both arms vigorously. I took my foot off the accelerator, rolled slowly to a stop.

The anxious face that peered through my side window was dark and rough with beard. I bit my lip. Under any ordinary circumstances I would have refused to let a strange man in. Today, with the temperature in the single digits, ordinary caution was first cousin to murder.

I popped the lock, and he joined me, bringing a blast of Arctic air with him.

"I'm Jeff Kourahan," he said, pulling down his scarf to give me a good look at him. "I appreciate your stopping."

"Cindy," I said, setting the car slowly into motion again. "Cynthia Appledon."

"The old lady's daughter," he said, rubbing his hairy cheeks. "People wondered," Jeff paused, "why you hadn't come." He looked out his window. I wouldn't have picked him for a local. His knit cap, scarf, and quilted coat were what everyone wore, but obviously new.

"I was out of the country," I said shortly. "On business." In Greece, to be precise, leading a group of tourists around the ancient sites, telling new versions of old stories, and arguing with bus drivers and hotel desk clerks.

He nodded, well-I-knew-that, and I suppressed a spurt of annoyance. Three Corners is a small place, without too many secrets. The sole proprietor of Classic Tours, Inc., I come home twice a year for a month or so, travel the ancient world the rest of the time. It's a good living, and advance compensation for—

The car hit an icier patch, slued. I turned the wheels, tapped the accelerator and recovered. At Three Corners, a church, a store, and a half-dozen houses at a "y" in the road, I crunched to a stop in front of Barney's General Purpose. Tourists find Barney's quaint. Natives know its tight-packed clutter is born of necessity. There are no quick trips to Championberg once the winter sets in. The store has a public phone.

Hand on the doorlatch, Jeff cocked his head at me, weighing his words. "I've taken the house a quarter mile beyond your mother's. I'd save me a good deal of trouble if you just take me on." Our taxi service is intermittent. Jack Chauvenet doesn't like to turn out in bad weather.

I put my hands at ten and two on the wheel. A quarter mile beyond my mother's meant he'd rented Stone House. If Tom Wheeler trusted him with his property, Kourahan was trustworthy indeed. Wheelers are cautious to a fault, have been for two hundred years and more. I shrugged, set the car rolling again, past the white wood columns of the village church.

"Thanks," Jeff said, then, hesitant, "You may not have heard. I've been doing a little dairying. Come May, I'll be opening a shop for the summer trade. I'm up here getting the new nannies settled, going over the place."

He was milking goats. I nodded, mind mostly on the car's uneasy motion, remembering a black kid climbing an olive tree, flecks of sunlight dancing on twig-littered ground, a sharp, feral scent. There'd been a distant clamor on the breeze, a dog barking and someone beating on a pan.

"I've named it 'The Greenwife.'"

Startled, I glanced at him, but he was lost in his own vision of herbed cheeses and happy tourists, a hand-carved sign and a steady trade with the New York gourmet stores. Coaxing the car up Henderson's Hill, I bit my lip thoughtfully. Jeff's woman of wooden leaves, flowers, and fruit was not—

"Look," the male voice said softly.

Caught in the level sunbeams, the icy maples at the crest were a glory of ebony, crystal, and gold. I drove straight into the glare, trusting my memory that the road did not curve until the foot of the hill. Jeff twisted to look back, but I didn't dare glance in the rearview mirror as the car slithered in the ruts.

The snow was pink in the evening sun's light, lavender in the shadows, when I turned into my mother's drive and stopped short. Jeff would have to walk from here. The car would never make the long slope to Stone House. He gathered himself together, put his hand on the door handle, said, "Shovel your walk?"

I nodded yes. I'd picked my clothes for the plane and the city. My high-heeled boots would make it awkward getting to the snow shovel that leaned beside the mailbox in the closed porch, and my thin gloves would be a complete loss after five minutes' work.

He got out, and I switched off the engine and pulled the lapels of my coat across. They sold gas at Three Corners, but this time of year it was hard for the truck to come. I must not waste what I had. There was no telling if my mother had laid in her winter supplies. There were a few items that always required a trip to Championberg and she didn't get around anymore.

I rolled one cold shoulder and then the other, trying to ignore the steady scrap of metal on icy stone, the fact that there was nothing but frost at the window panes. Just this summer Mother's curious, welcoming face would have peered out as soon as any car pulled into the drive.

When Jeff stashed the shovel on the porch and came over, I lowered my window, and said, "Thanks."

Want me to wait while you check things out?"

I shook my head. "It'll be dark soon. You should be getting home." I knew what I was going to find. I wanted to be alone with it.

He squinted at me, mouth full of unasked questions, then decided to take me at my word.

"Thanks," I said again, for that, and for the cleared path.

"Welcome," he said, having already picked up the sparse local conversational style. He strode away, not hasty but making good time, a broad-shouldered figure with a giant's shadow.

I rolled the car window up. Probably on his way to a warm supper prepared by a wife or girlfriend newly-elevated to business partner. My breath blurred him out of existence, even as I imagined what the woman must be like. Short and dark, with fake tortoiseshell earrings and a husky laugh, or tall and blond in a pale blue sweater—

I looked at the silent house while the frost grew feathers and needles across the windshield. The car ticked, cooling. I hitched my coat tighter around me, watching the few clouds fleeing west turn ruddy then ashen. The wind was rising. By morning the autumn's first snow would look new-fallen again.

When two or three stars appeared on the eastern horizon, I got out cautiously, slid the slick soles of my boots along the walk. I could freeze to death if I fell out here. The bare-limbed bushes chattered in a gust of wind as I eased myself up the steps. The sheltered porch seemed almost warm as I fished my spare house key from my purse.

Half a dozen humidifiers sat purring on the living room floor. Mother must have arranged for someone trustworthy to come in and refill them, check the furnace, do what little needed to be done for her. I'd have to find out who. They'd have a key to the house I'd have to reclaim. I unwound my scarf, unbuttoned my coat, hung both on empty pegs in the entryways, and then left my foolish boots leaning one against the other.

I looked in every room as I passed, sockinged feet padding on the bare boards. The house looked unoccupied, rugs rolled up, furniture covered. All the windows were blind with frost. I called, "Mother?" and heard my voice whisper back from dusty corners. A mouse, driven in by the cold, fled under a bureau, peered out with beady eyes.

Unlatching the door to the back hall, I stopped. At the far end chipped stone posts framed a rectangle of total blackness. A cold breath of mold touched my face. It took an effort to move to the gaping hole and look in. "Mother?" I switched on the lights. The great tree rooted deep in the earthen floor didn't even rustle.

She'd settled in well. Already it took a sharp eye to see the human form in the trunk and upraised branches. The bole that had been a face was healed over, closed. Its nostrils, mouth, and eyes stopped forever. There would be some consciousness still. Grandmother's apple-blossom hair quivered with muffled song days before her daughter went to walk the hills, singing in the spring.

I looked up at the shuttered skylight, sat down on the step formed by the end of the flooring. An ancient tune droned in my head as I tried to think. Tomorrow, or maybe the next day, I would check the arrangements for the house. I had twenty, twenty-five, possibly thirty years until my own greening.

The furnace switched on with a rumble.

I drove my nails into the palm of my hand.

It was not fair, the loss, of freedom, of ordinary pleasures, of my *self*. I reached down and pressed my bleeding flesh against the cold soil of the winter room, remembering rocky hills and bold blue seas, doomed fish glittering in the net, and a whiff of laurel on the wind.

At the end of summer the whole house would have

smelled of dry grass and sun-baked dust. Naked, her beautiful hair flowing past the narrow waist that childbirth hadn't taken from her, Mother had come here and embraced the tree, serenely confident that I would come home, tend the tree and wait my turn.

I pressed my stocking-covered toes into the cool, crumbling earth. The local legends call us greenwives. "A simple corruption of 'goodwife,' one tourist had told me, and I had nodded and smiled polite agreement. It was hard to imagine—

"Cindy? Ms. Appledon?" I hadn't paid much attention to him, but I certainly knew the muffled voice. Jeff Kourahan. I staggered as I stood. I must not have relocked the front door. "Jeff?" Feet thudding on bare boards, I ran to intercept him. "What are you doing here?"

Key in hand, he stood in the entryway. Seeing my anger, he flushed. "I thought you might need some company, or at least some dinner." He offered the heavy bag in the crook of his arm. "I did say I'd been looking after things."

"Oh," I said, deflated. Busy with driving and my own thoughts, I'd missed that. I fumbled for some way to depreciate my anger without losing moral ground. "You should have knocked."

"I did. Hard. Several times."

"Oh," I said again. Then, expecting him to apologize, "You startled me."

His jaw lifted a stubborn fraction. I said abruptly, "Go into the kitchen. I'll be right along." Hands shaking, I closed the door to the back hall, carefully shutting in the cold, moldy smell. Perhaps Mother had simply told him she was going away for a bit and asked him to care for things.

Perhaps not. I licked blood and earth from my palm. My mother had always been discreet, but when you green you are in the grip of uncontrollable needs. If Mother had said or shown too much—I pressed my hand to my quivering lips. She should have sent for me. I would have come. I'd told her that.

I walked into the kitchen just as Jeff turned the overhead light on. Row after row, jewel-like, preserves filled the shelves around the walls. I could count the days and weeks before Mother's greening. There were no pears, no apples. This autumn the birds would have eaten their fill in our trees and the deer feasted on windfalls.

Jeff piled his coat, hat, and gloves on the table beside his sack, lifted out a bottle of wine, a cloth-wrapped cheese. There was dark, curling hair at the neck of his shirt, and I could smell his musky maleness. I stood, blind and deaf, trying to think of a way to ask how much he had seen, what he knew.

"Cynthia?" A dark-nailed hand, gentle but firm, lifted my chin. I stared. Jeff was a handsome man, with black eyes and a proud, curving nose, but that was not what drew my eyes. Above the smooth sweep of his forehead, among the curls pressed flat by his knitted hat, there were twin knobs of horn.

Silently, he laughed at the round "o" of my mouth.

I turned to flee, my heart filled with the proper joyous terror.

He held me in place with his free hand on my shoulder. "Once more," he said, giving me a little shake, making sure of my attention, "have you got any wineglasses?"

"In there," I said, pointing with a glance.

He released me.

I stared at tear-blurred purple plums and golden apricots, thinking of one hot noon when I crouched in the shade of a marble pillar. I had wanted to believe that someone was hiding in the shifting shadows, safe from merely human vision, but I knew there was no one there and never would be.

But he had merely been further out of sight.

I had truly come home.

Jeff uncorked the bottle, poured, tasted. He gestured with his head and glass for me to take up mine, then lifted his own. He spilled a few drops and said, sharp teeth flashing white in his beard, "This for the future, that for the past, the very gods marvel at what's come to pass."

Together, we drank the sea-dark wine.

Blood Moon

T he Dame sat on her balcony, hands folded, white lap pelt in place. Every day, all day, she kept watch on what happened within the Fastness. At night, the watchdogs were unchained. Now they slept in their kennel near the gate, heaps of russet, ash, and charcoal fur. By day, the Dame kept watch within the keep.

It was Blood Moon, halfway between the winter solstice and the spring equinox. Nearly a hundred seasons ago, the stone circle that marked the eight festivals had been pulled down, so no one could be certain of the exact day. Soon, the Dame was sure.

Now, although the high pastures were green, cold rain pelted down. Hail had rattled on the courtyard paving earlier. The old took the long way around, under the porticos, to stay dry and warm. The young were indoors, set to work. The Dame sighed. It had been a dull day with nothing to do but worry.

Children tried to evade her keen eye. Adolescents saw the Dame as an old busybody. Older people had a better understanding of her worth. Her contemporaries were envious or wary, depending on how wise they were themselves.

Knowledge is power. Secrets more powerful still. The Dame knew many. Hammett, Wenna's son, was not her husband's boy, but his brother's. Three of the kitchen staff were pilfering from the storerooms. The captain of the guard slipped down to the gate after dark every seventh night and stood, listening. Sometimes he spoke a word or two.

Since there was no cure for a sterile husband but a discreet agreement, the first was probably laudable. There were so few babies. Because food might be short this year, the second was not yet important but could be. The fields were too muddy to plant, even if the cold broke soon. However, given that there was no good reason anyone talked with anything that lived beyond the walls of the Fastness, the last was important. There were things outside that wanted in.

The Mother and the Maiden must know. I have delayed, the Dame thought and stroked the white fur. The other two would want to act. She sighed, thinking, *I have waited long enough.* "Such matters are not for you alone," a voice long dead reminded her.

It was early, but no one was abroad. Best to get on with it. The Dame wrapped her pelt about her and rose, stiff with long sitting. Aided by her cane, she hobbled into her sitting room. A hot tisane would be welcome, even if her evening meal had not been brought up.

Elowin was a marvel, for although there was no supper yet, there were three thick slices of bread under an over-turned bowl on a plate, a toasting fork, and a pot of honey. Raspberry tea was in the caddy on the mantle piece. Her jug was full of spring water. The hearth glowed.

The Dame sat the kettle on the hob and barred the door. She went to her privy chamber and stripped off. One hand on the back of a heavy chair, she worked slowly until her muscles were supple and she could work free standing. Then she did thrusts and blocks with her cane.

She washed and anointed herself with rosemary oil. Rinsing everything so that no scent of sweat remained she emptied the basin down the shaft. The Dame's personal privy was a necessary luxury. Just how capable she was physically was something she didn't share.

In fresh-aired clothes, she unbarred the door, settled to brewing tea and toasting bread. Putting the last slice onto the hearth-warmed plate, she heard Elowin on the stairs. "Butter," said the serving girl as she came in. "Dinner will be late. The salt beef's still tough."

The Dame smiled.

Elowin grinned. "If he'd just set it to simmer early. It's a bad season for game." The girl looked sober. "It's a bad season to be out of the Fastness, if you ask me. People talk about how old and thick the walls are. To me, that says they worry about them."

Yes. The Dame nodded and reached for the butter crock, thinking, *Now she will tell me.* Elowin was thoughtful, but she could just as well have left the butter on her first trip up the spiral stair. She'd wanted a few minutes with the Dame.

"The cows wouldn't go out to graze this morning."

"Why was that? Tea?"

"No," said the girl. "Thank you. I had buttermilk in the kitchen. I've been at the churning. It's a good batch. You can taste the early clover is up."

The Dame poured a cup for herself. Its steam formed restless ghosts. She asked again, "Why wouldn't the cows go out?"

"No one knew."

The Dame looked up from her cup, alert. The girl was not yet old enough to be a dairymaid, but she helped cut the curds and turn the cheeses. Elowin was perceptive and more inclined to listen than to talk: reasons the Dame favored her.

"They were frightened. At first the herd master decided to bring them into the stone folds when they wouldn't let down. Even with the calves right with them, they were hard to milk. Now he's bringing them home."

The click as the Dame put down her cup seemed loud, even against the steady drumming of the rain. The night was going to be wet and windy. *Blood Moon*, she thought, *when dormant things wake.*

"The herders and the dogs had all they could do to keep them on the road." The girl's eyes were cloudy with fear. "They got them into the fold at Second Switchback. There wasn't time to send for food. They drank what the calves didn't want, stripped the rest into the dirt."

31

"Why wasn't there time?"

"No one will travel in the dark. They'll bring the goats down the day after tomorrow, if they can."

"Why didn't the herd master send word?" That she, the Dame, not know there was trouble in the high pastures was as worrying as the news itself. Herders were used to lonely pastures and the cows' instincts were sound. The goats, half-wild, couldn't be gathered in haste, but the Fastness could not afford to lose them.

Elowin looked away. "There was howling. Far away and then near. Eyes said he saw tracks. Like a wolf's. Bigger than his hand." She looked back. "The herders argued a lot. Then they took that for a bad sign."

Wolves. There hasn't been a wolf here for a generation. "If Kenver saw something, it was there. Why didn't they move the herd?"

"They moved from South Peak to West, two days ago, without sending word. Drove the cows and the goats across the Neck. Then they rebuilt the Gate of Sarsens." She looked into the scarlet coals, finding the truth there. "Well, they pulled four stones into place and closed the road. Now they're coming home." The girl's voice shook on the last word.

The Gate of Sarsens. The stones held power. A hundred years ago the people of Fastness had broken the circle to use its sarcens to close the road from the peaks. When that need passed they had pulled the stones aside but had not rebuilt the circle. It took ox teams to move sarsens. The Fastness had fewer oxen every year.

Indeed, there were fewer people now than there had been when the circle was broken. Fields were fallow from lack of plowmen and teams. If the herdsmen had moved four of the "silent giants," whatever they feared was more than matter of a stray wolf and the dairy herds. The Dame asked, "When did you hear this?"

"This afternoon." The girl gestured at the food. "I thought—"

"Yes. Well done." The Dame lifted her tea, paused, then put it down. "Tell the war master I'd like to see him. Don't let anyone hear you. Before full night is soon enough."

The girl went: quick and silent.

War Master Tremain was past active duty, but he would understand there was no time to explain, to argue, to reach a consensus. People would have to be swept into action.

I was not worried enough, thought the Dame, and stroked the white pelt in her lap, soothing herself. Once darkness had fallen, there would be much to do. She could only hope that the war master had been receiving news she had not.

Tremain was prompt, if out of breath. Stout and smelling of the stables, he sat without invitation and listened. "No," he said. "I hadn't heard." He frowned but did not speculate. "The walls are sound. The people trained. We are the Fastness; we can defend. That much I have made sure of. But we need more."

"Then there will be more," said the Dame. Between them, they outlined a plan. Then War Master Tremain rose. "I'll send the other two, separately."

The Dame nodded.

Well after dark, what might have been three huge wolves—a black, a red, and a white—met at the gate of the Fastness. They nosed around and loped into the shadows near the kennel. All the guard dogs whined, once. The patter of the rain rose and fell. Once a spurt of sleet rattled on paving. Torches burned down and fell, hissing in the puddles.

The Fastness was always dark and still at night. People who rise at dawn go to bed not long after sundown. They let walls protect them, not sentinels. Midnight, and the captain appeared, walking as though there were no rain. He went to the gate, lifted its three massive bolts, and slid back its bar.

Then he waited, empty-eyed, his sodden clothes black by waning torchlight.

Alert, the three crouched. Like wolves, they bared their teeth when something began to open the gate. Without bothering to glance over his shoulder, the captain of the guard slipped out. There was an odd noise, then nothing.

The three rose and padded to the gap in the Fastness defenses. Something, roused from its eating, snarled at them. Dog-like, the three quietly backed away. Unlike dogs, once inside they stood on their hind legs, pushed the gate closed, and took off their pelts.

Swiftly and silently, the three women rebarred it and dropped the bolts. The captain would not be coming home. They gathered their pelts around them, ready to go their ways. Then the oak panel creaked as something heavy hit it from the outside. The bolts groaned and the bar shuddered.

The Dame handed her white fur to the Mother, the Mother handed her red pelt to the Maiden, who draped it over her own black one. The Dame, clothed in nothing but shadows and light, drew her cane from hiding. The other two fled to call the guard and wake the keep.

Every dog in the Fastness howled as the Dame opened the gate and stood in the opening. In her left hand was a sword and in her right the cane-sheath. *It's been a good beginning*, she thought. *If it must be, let it be a good end.* "See me!" she shouted.

Seeing her, the thing reared back. It dripped the red of blood over the white of bone and the black of dung. "Sister," it hissed at her, "do you not know me?"

"I do," said the Dame. "You are the one who came before me."

"I can name you!" it said.

"So you can," said the Dame, "for you knew me as Maiden and Mother."

"I am the many in one," it cried, in a different voice. The wailing of the guard dogs was terrible.

"Sister, you may have me," said the Dame. The guard dogs' silence was more terrible still.

The thing billowed like flames, although the rain fell straight down.

"You may have me," said the Dame, and sheathed her sword cane. "I come." She cast the cane behind her.

"No!" said the figure, in yet another voice. "It will be too many!"

"You may have me!"

"No! We will die the real death!" cried many voices, all together.

"You must take me!" said the Dame and strode into the other. There was a vast silence. Something stood there, flickering uncertainly. It drew in on itself with a sound like fire eating wood. Livid lightning leaped from earth to sky. Thunder smote the smoking earth and echoed everywhere.

The Mother held the Maiden and both wept, but they were the only ones who mourned. They, and the wailing dogs, who did not know what had happened, but knew a creature akin to them was gone. The people of the Fastness shouted as one for joy.

In the courtyard the air was still, but high above the clouds fled on a swift wind, and the night's pale eye looked down. In moonlight the new Dame took her place on her balcony. In moonlight the new Mother spoke to the people, choosing the father-to-be of her first child. In moonlight there were beginnings and an ending.

Softly at first, then more loudly, women's fingers brushed drumheads, and the men did the slow dances that mark the passing of someone rich in years. Then the men tapped the drums and the women danced the fast dances that celebrate a new Dame and a new Mother.

At dawn there came the cry of a newborn girl. She was wrapped in the pelt of the Maiden and so sanctified it. They took the black fur, shook it out, warmed it before the fire, and wrapped startled Elowin in it. *You won't forget me*, said a voice deep in her mind. No, answered the Maiden, knowing the other would whisper in her dreams. On her shoulders, her pelt shivered.

The Decisive Princess

T here was once a barbaric king, who, aspiring to be well-thought-of by his more civilized neighbors—the source of goods which the king resold at an extraordinary markup further north—instituted a novel method for dealing with those guilty of crimes against the state. He combined elements of southern law with his own thoughts in such a way that he could, with pride, show the resulting spectacle to envoys. In this manner he provided both an entertainment and a not-too-subtle assurance that he was under their sway, something that he had no intention of allowing to happen.

His method was to place the accused traitor into the arena that his southern neighbors had been happy to construct for him. It had cost not much more than three times what the same contractors would have charged had it been built on their own territory supplying their own laborers, instead of in his territory using his farm folk in their off-season. The contractors and their sponsors thought the king was not aware of this and he did not disabuse them of their notion.

The accused had to choose between two huge soundproof doors. Behind one was a fighting bull, pricked and goaded to the highest pitch of fury. Behind the other was a lady of the nobility, perhaps not the prettiest or the most accomplished—for those wed early—but nonetheless of good education, breeding, and with a substantial dowry, her gift from the king for accepting an arranged marriage instead of one of her own choosing. She was always a woman who would be a fit wife for an ambitious man, a woman whose family would see to their son-in-law's success—and his loyalty.

The barbarian king had but one child, a daughter, who he had caused to be reared in every way as a prince. It was his intention that she, in due course, be the linchpin of a suitable alliance, yet defend her interests and those of her people against those of her husband and his folk. A fine match was in negotiation for a prince from the south, one second in line to a throne. In those days, when life was quite uncertain, such a one was a man of excellent prospects that might be improved by some judicious pruning of his family tree.

However, to bring the match to fruition, the king knew, his daughter must be delivered to her future husband a virgin, for such was the fashion of the southern lands where inheritance went from father to son. For a man to be certain a woman's child was of his own flesh he must marry a virgin and keep her from all other men. The king, who was king because he was a sister's son to the former king, had his doubts about this, knowing women and their ways, but if politics dictated that his daughter remain chaste, chaste she would be.

With the southern monarch's envoys already sighted on the road, he found the princess deep in private conversation with a handsome, poor, and doubtless ambitious warlord who came from farther north than the king was certain his own power extended. The northern border was always a troublesome area, where it was often wisest to simply overlook various things as long as fealty was sworn. Nonetheless, the king declared this might-be lover an oath-breaking traitor and condemned him to the trial of the arena.

To the great wonder of the court and populace, his daughter, more prince than princess, made no complaint and the king, emboldened by her silence, selected as the young man's prospective bride one of her handmaidens, one whose favors the monarch had often sought and failed to win. It was his thought that, once married, the wife might be persuadable where the maid was not. Those the king found inconvenient often had bad fortune and it was whispered that his reach was not short of his grasp and his grasp was often deadly.

It was with pleasant anticipation that the king took his place of honor at the arena. The only blot on the day was that his daughter chose to appear veiled from head to toe. Being no fool, he had her drape back the black gauze for an instant that he, loving father that he was, might be sure of her. She had only one ring, a fine ruby much like the ones he wore, and that she toyed with restlessly. Her face, though calm, was pale as ivory, and her ebon eyes were lustrous, as if with unshed tears. In her saffron gown and gold-worked scarlet girdle, backed by the black cloud of her veil, she was stunning. The king heard the envoys—who had not seen the prize for which they bargained—murmur appreciation.

Presently, as the pomp and ceremony that might precede a funeral or a bridal went forward, the king became absorbed in delightful thoughts of the future. Serving girls came and went, bringing sweetmeats, wine, and sherbets. The southern envoys chatted among themselves, making complimentary remarks on the anticipated spectacle, comments that they intended to be overheard. The king, pleased, lolled against his cushions, waiting for the fanfare that would herald the moment of decision.

When it came, the might-be lover and therefore-possible traitor stood forth barefoot, in tunic and short cloak, weaponless. The king knew a moment of regret that events must play out as they would, for the man excited much favorable comment among the female companions of the envoys. Southern princes were reputedly soft with the comforts and lax ways of the south, not to mention that several were known to have handsome, painted pageboys in their households—

His daughter was not a woman to be happy with a man who was less than virile and there was, there always had been, that weakness on the northern border of his kingdom. However, the duties of a ruler often require that the joys of the marriage bed be, at best, tepid. Even as the king mused on his own marriage, which had produced only one child before his wife retired, permanently, to her own rooms under the protection of her own guards, the trumpets sounded again.

The king saw, in the corner of his eye, his daughter make a tiny decisive movement, and he smiled in his beard. She was indeed a prince. He had expected she would know how the lots had fallen. The monarch had not bothered to find out since either outcome was pleasing to him. The right door it was then. Had she chosen to see her lover trampled and impaled by the enraged bull? Or had she chosen a lifetime of seeing another woman, one who had been subject to her, have the man she might have desired?

Men pulled the ropes that opened the chosen door: it was the bull that came, snorting and stamping. The king felt a great satisfaction that his daughter was as tough-minded as he, a satisfaction that turned to bewilderment as the young man took off his cape and waved it at the beast, which charged the piece of red cloth. The man whipped his cloak up and out of the way as the bull thundered by. It wheeled in a cloud of dust, looking for a target for its pain and rage.

Again the man waved his cape, and the crowd roared as the bull passed the man by, futilely attempting to hook the fluttering thing with its horns. A third time the scene was repeated, and by then the entire crowd was upon its feet, beating upon the railings in excitement. Not least among them the southern envoys the king wished to impress. "The gods speak!" cried one and then cried all.

The king stared, uncertain how to retrieve the victim from the arena, for retrieved he must be, with the envoys as witnesses. "Father," said his daughter, and she knelt before him as if to plead for mercy. He sighed with relief: she would help him by letting him be the indulgent father rather than the strict monarch. "Yes," he said and bent close to listen.

She laid her hands, the hands he has so often held when she was a child, upon his. The king felt a sting. His arm went numb, to the elbow, to the shoulder, then to the heart. He who had had taught his daughter *all* the ways of princes, sagged back against his cushions, dying.

The crowd, enthralled by the spectacle in the arena, saw nothing. His daughter rose, raised her arms, flinging wide the black veil so it obscured any view of the king. She stood forth at the railing next to the royal standard, proud in saffron and scarlet, and gestured. The left-hand door, the door that supposedly hid the bride-to-be, opened, man-wide and no further, then closed behind the northern warlord.

The dusty, blood-streaked beast gored the un-yielding planks. Finally, fury spent, it ambled down the passage to its stall. As the bull went on its way, the princess rested one long-fingered hand upon her scarlet girdle and smiled. It could stay, muzzle in manager, until it was sacrificed at the old King's funeral feast, a feast that would also be her wedding banquet, for behind the gold-worked silk of her girdle lay a future queen of her people or lord of his father's. She would have a secure northern border and the man she desired.

For all the new queen's tears as a serving girl discovered her father's fatal accident with his ring, some were thoughtful. The lady's composure when the northern warlord knelt and offered his condolences, his gratitude for his salvation, and accepted her offer of her hand in marriage was noticed by some. However, the wise majority paid no attention at all, for they remembered the ways of the dead king, her father, and knew that the princess *had* been reared as a prince.

As for the southern envoys, they went home to their court with nothing to show for their embassy, except for the whispered observation of the most senior of them in their king's ear, that it would be as well to be on good terms with those barbarians to the north, for they were nearly as clever as civilized men, far more ruthless, and reckless to a degree never seen in the south, for they dared to be ruled by a woman.

In appreciation of Frank R. Stockton's "The Lady, or the Tiger," and with the observation that, being a man, he was wise to end his story before the princess made her choice.

The End
of
the Dream Time

That's what I brought you to see. That big gray honeycomb the air makes a little noise in as it passes through. It's an eerie old thing to look at, isn't it? But maybe it looks like just another wind-carved rock to you, not that different from half the stuff up at this end of the canyon.

Bet you wonder why I had you walk all this way in the heat when we could have talked sitting in the shadow of the council house or out in the low fields digging roots with the rest. But I've brought all the children of the families here to see it, and now it's your turn.

Well, sit down in the shade while I have my say, and then we'll go back.

Look at it. I've been up here on windy days when it howled like it was alive and in pain. Winter nights, sometimes, when there's a storm from the west you can hear it in the village, so far away you'd take it for a feral dog if you didn't know.

Any of your cousins ever talk to you about it? No? Well, we kind of keep the knowing for the grownups. One day it'll be worn away. I don't know what they'll point to for warning then. Maybe it won't matter.

It was different here once. There was more water in the creek, and plants grew wild all along the canyon. Every spring all the young ones had to go out and pull them by the handfuls to make sure the corn reached its full height.

We hated it—it left you tired at night, and your hands got all green with the sap. It was a good life, even though I was too young to know it. Things were good here, better than the best season you've ever seen, or are likely to see.

Maybe so. I wouldn't mind being wrong.

Let me get on with this. It was my cousin Georgiana who saw it first. She was more spirited than most, a good worker, although some grownups called her flighty. When she'd pulled enough weeds—

They're the plants you don't want.

Nothing, just throw them away to dry up.

I said, things were different.

As I was saying, when she'd pulled enough weeds to satisfy Old Farnam—he was in charge of this section of farms—

We had fields right up through here and beyond, clear up to the Whitson's gap.

Yep. Well, when Georgiana'd pulled enough to feel sure she could satisfy Farnam that she was entitled to a break, she climbed up on the rim, right there, where there's a notch.

No particular reason, I expect. Just to look around. There'd be a bit more of a breeze up there, and you could see the hawks hunting, riding the wind up from the canyon, watching the rim grass for rabbits and snakes.

Something like a quail, but they ate—

Now I want you to listen to this and not keep interrupting me. I'll explain things like that after. There's enough hard ideas coming without picking away at the meaning of this word and that.

Georgiana was up there, looking around, maybe flipping a pebble or two back into the river, when she saw a cloud, flying across the wind, coming from the Black Mountains.

That way.

Well, we'd have to climb up there.

Not today.

Maybe when it's cooler.

If you can get him to, it's all right with me, but we're not doing it right now.

Don't you go sulky on me. This is important. You're always wanting to be more grownup, now's your chance.

No, she couldn't tell what it was. Georgie just knew it wasn't anything that should be where it was, doing what it was, and it was coming right at her, fast. I suppose if she'd had time she would have skinned down out of there and run home, but she didn't.

She hunkered down in the rocks right there in that notch.

I said, if Tim'll take you, you can go, but not with me, and not today. I'm too stiff in the joints to go climbing around for no reason.

Well, *I've* seen it, and I'm telling you about it.

That thing came gusting in and settled right there where the honeycomb is, but it didn't look like that then. It looked like—see that cloud over there, the one with two bumps on top and a flat bottom?—like that, but solid, like cotton fluff. A clever thing. We probably wouldn't have noticed it if Georgiana hadn't happened to have been there.

I've always wondered if it mightn't have been around for a while.

Well.

Georgie said the whole thing just sat there, shimmering, for a little while, then sort of oozed in on itself and turned into big sky-boulder, as pitted and black as the piece in the council house. She could not believe her eyes, and she wasn't about to go up to the thing and touch it. Might be something dangerous. She got herself back down, quiet as a mouse, and ran for home.

We all came up and had a look at it.

We didn't trust it. It was unnatural. Who'd believe an enormous rock like that would fall out of the sky without making a sound, or leaving a hole in the ground bigger than our village? Grandfather's cousin, Jay Hmoung, said a meteor that size should have left bits and pieces behind it for a day's walk and more. We searched all around and found nothing—

I think maybe something was already inside, watching. Gives me a funny feeling to think about it now. I was one of the boys set to hunt around it, up close, looking for scorch marks, or burns, or anything that would show that huge thing hadn't just been set in place, like an egg on a tabletop.

I wasn't scared. I should have been—would have been, if I had any sense—but I wasn't.

I believe you. But sometimes it's better to be a little frightened.

Okay. There it was, and there it sat, and we were sure it wasn't natural, but we couldn't figure how, what, and why it had come to be. It worried everybody for a while, even if they didn't believe Georgiana's story.

Oh, yeah, there were plenty of doubters.

A lot figured she'd been asleep, hadn't noticed the stone when she climbed into the notch, then, confused by the changes when she woke up, half-dreamed what she told us. A few said she'd lied to cover up that she'd been sleeping, even though she wasn't on watch. Almost nobody wanted to believe she'd told the simple truth.

They didn't mean any harm. It was just a more comfortable sort of thought. You get older and find out people mostly don't like to face strange things. A cloud that turned into a rock—

Well, maybe you won't. I hope not. Someone has to do some thinking around here.

Even if we weren't all that happy about it, there was always work to do. We went back to the business of scratching a living, and everything went along about the way it always had. For a while.

I was getting old enough that they expected me to help with the hunting. I didn't mind. I was good at it, and it was like a day off. If I made it back with six rabbits or so, or a dozen quail, they counted it time well spent, no matter what I'd done with the rest of the day.

Nope, that wasn't even very many. There was more water then. A hunter could count on finding small game. It was a bad night when we didn't have meat in camp.

Yeah, well, so do I. So do I. Some nights we had a half a rabbit apiece—could have had more, but it would have been a waste. We ate green corn, then, too. Didn't wait for the harvest.

Just planted a bit more, is all.

I know.

I told you, I was out hunting. It was no accident that I doubled over to here. Farnam liked us to keep an eye on the thing, and we mostly made a point of just happening by, if it wasn't too far out of our way.

So I was the first to see it.

You should have wanted to know that already. Ask important questions first. Suppose it *was* dangerous, there might be something you needed to do.

Remember when you learned to sling stones? You had to learn how to pick out a pebble and how to hit something. Then you had to learn how to find a rabbit? Then you had to learn how to hit a rabbit. Learning how to handle an emergency is something like that. You have to learn all the pieces—

All right, I'll get on with it.

When I came near the rock I could see that there was something moving around outside, picking up bits of this and that and putting them down again. I dropped flat on my belly in the bushes.

It hadn't. I don't know why. I hadn't been especially careful, just come jogging in with my backload of rabbits, wanting to take a quick look and get on back to the village. It *should* have seen me—

It was as big as that boulder over there, the brown one I could just about touch the top of if I stood real tall.

It wasn't ugly. If it had looked more like us, I might have thought it was, but rabbits, quail, and snakes are just themselves. This was like that. Just something else. Six-legged. Or four-legged if you counted the things it stood on as legs, and called the other pair arms. There's drawings in the council house. You'll see them.

I crawled all the way to the second rim gap on my stomach, then got up and ran to tell Old Farnam. He told the headwoman—

It was a woman in those days.

Your mother has a lot to teach you if you think that.

Time will tell. Her name was Shirilee, and she got all the elders together fast as she could. It didn't take long before they decided the first thing they needed was more information. They sent me back.

I wasn't scared the first time, but the second time I'd listened to what the council members said to one another. They sure weren't making any assumption that whatever-it-was was friendly. It was an open secret that the elders knew a good bit they didn't talk about, kept things from the youngers.

So we wouldn't grow up afraid, I suppose.

I'll telling you now.

There wasn't anything stirring outside when I crept up, but what looked like a meteor had changed into the honeycomb you can see up there. Look at it. See all the hollow places, bigger than a tall man? They were capped and closed, each filled with things like the first whatever-it-was I'd seen, except they were all small, soft-looking, and white.

I took my time watching. Presently I was sure there was nothing stirring, and I got up and went walking around, not at all worried about the thing I'd seen. I was feeling pretty bold, looking forward to having the elders' attention when I told my story.

Until I nearly stepped on it. Or what was left of it. Skin, mostly. It was lying there on the ground like an old worn-out glove, sagging in on itself. The bottle-flies were at it already, and the crows had eaten the eyes.

It hummed and heaved and shifted a bit. For a moment, I thought it was alive like that. Made my stomach turn over. I nearly retched my guts up, crouching in the shade of the nearest bush, too sick to find better cover. When I finished, I looked up—

No, I'm all right.

When I looked up, all those soft white things had turned in their cells, and they were all staring at me. All those pale, blind-looking eyes, watching, watching *me*.

I ran so fast I didn't even know I'd cut my foot right through my moccasin until I got back to the village. When I finished babbling everything to the elders, they didn't even bother to vote, just started out for here without another word, even though it was near dark.

I couldn't go with them, but everyone who could came up here that very night, and gathered every bit of dry wood and brush they could find. Made a pile taller than a tall man, all the way around.

Set fire to it.

The cells popped in the heat, and the things inside came out writhing, fell down into the fire, tried to crawl out, died sizzling. Everything but that stony bit up there could burn, and did, burned for three nights and two days. We kept guards on it all that time, and the young ones ran back and forth, bringing firewood.

I was a little bit of a hero.

Until the next rains didn't come.

See, one of the things the eldest hadn't even told the elders was exactly how we came to be here. You've sung the song yourself, so you know that, time was, we were up there among the stars, traveling to new homes.

I don't know; I was never there myself. I'm telling you what they told me. It was a big fight, us and them, out there between here and some other place. We never saw who they were. Maybe we lost and maybe we won, but the boat we were on—

Like Jay's skiff, but bigger, and closed.

Metal, I think.

The *Illyrion*.

That's a *name*, not a thing.

We—not us of course, but our great-great's and great-great-great's—crashed down yonder. They expected to be killed by the fall, but they skidded in, every one knocked out cold. When they found they were alive they came out of their boat—

Oh, it was big, bigger than three or four council houses all made into one.

They came out of their boat to have a look around. It was pretty badly smashed, so they carried a good deal of what they had out, planning to shelter in a cave, use some of the boat's metal for a big panel to close it off.

That's right, the big one in the east cliff. They never did make that door. When they were all out, the *Illyrion* exploded for no reason they could figure out. Vaporized is more like it. There was almost nothing left. They were stuck—

Jay'll tell you more about that, some other time. That's his part of the story. I'm telling you my part.

Every one of us can recite some of it, so we won't forget.

Now I want you to listen to me carefully. At first, they thought they had just been lucky to survive, and luckier still they'd moved enough stuff out of the *Illyrion* that they could do a little farming and even have enough to eat while they waited for the crops to bear.

They had hopes that one of the other star-boats would come and take them away, back to where they came from, or on to where they were going. But time went by, and what with one thing and another, they gave up on that. Mostly the oldest just died out and their hopes died with them.

If the eldest thought they were just fortunate, their youngers weren't so sure, especially once they saw that thing.

It got talked about. It might have been one of them, the ones that shot us down. Might have.

We talked about it a lot. Some of us began to wonder if maybe we were put here. To be watched. By the whatever-it-was. Maybe when it died, none of the rest of them wanted to bother—

It's a hard idea, I know.

You're shivering, you've heard enough for one day. Let's go back now. Mind you, you're not to scare your youngers with this. They'll never grow up venturesome if they hear it too early. That's why we wait. We have to stay strong.

No, that's the whole story. The rest's just details You'll come to know them like the rest of us. Any ideas you have, well, tell us. We've tried most things, but a fresh mind is always welcome.

Maybe it's just a silly notion, and everything's been a happenchance. Maybe the rains will come next season, and you'll see a hawk hunting quail in the rim grass, and we'll all eat green corn and rabbit until our bellies ache, and wonder why we worried so.

Just don't bet on it.

The Ragged Man

Hearing the clash of spear on shield, I woke staring into thinning mist. One willow branch was battering another in a quickening breeze. It was a night much like the one when I lay down on the moss under the overarching ferns and died.

I was a soldier, once, a captain in my duke's personal guard when he took his army to Carneze. The city hadn't paid its imposts, and was letting peasants live within its walls as freemen.

The heralds demanded entrance. When the city gate stayed closed the engineers broke it in with the lesser ram. Our orders were to invest without looting. No pillage meant no profits, and the sullen infantry took their anger out on the townspeople.

I and my troop rode in together, ignoring the screaming, leaving the ordering of the foot soldiers to their own officers. The duke's guard got first pick when there were pickings and were paid to stay disciplined when there were not. Our objective was to secure the blackened keep that rose over the tile roofs of the houses.

The old builders had a knack of locking block on block so the stones themselves fail before the join, but they hadn't perfected a way of holding gates without men. We pushed our way past servants with poles and kitchen knives, rode over the beds of herbs and flowers and dismounted at the door of the highest tower.

I went first. Up the stairs, into a room where the stink of potions and smokes hung heavy in the air. An age-twisted question mark of a man, bright-eyed and baleful, spread his arms to bar our way. Behind him, a veiled maiden caught up an ironbound chest, fumbled to loose its hasp as she glided away.

"Back off," I said, drawing my blade.

His lips moved, "Accursed, unclean—"

I swung my sword.

"May you never die until—" My blade connected. His body slumped to the floor. His head bounced and came to rest among tumbled books and pots, mouth agape with astonishment.

I laughed, then yelled we must find the maiden. The troop surged in pursuit. The chest lay broken in the room beyond, but the bearer was nowhere to be found. I thought it some witch-thing, dead with its master.

We scoured the tower of defenders, then went down into Carneze, ate food from pots tended by weeping women, went to sleep in beds whose owners lay heaped for the bone-fires.

A day's work, less dangerous than most.

It was the dead hour between midnight and dawn when I woke knowing I hadn't heard the watch change. Naked, I slid from between the sheets, cracked the shutter and looked down into the moonlit square. There was no jingle of harness, no tramp of guards. Ashes and bloodstains lay waiting for rain to erase them.

Nothing alive, yet the shadows moved.

We had not found the witch-girl.

And the ironbound chest had been broken open—

I sprang down the stairway to the stables. Arms around the snorting horse's neck, I rode through a maze of courtyards, leaned into the darkness by the doorpost to undo the latch. A shadow reached up, clawed at my side. My steed screamed and fled into the street, taking me with him.

The city was dead.

Warriors lay slumped in doorways, sprawled in gutters. Near the broken city gate, the Duke himself lay in the mud, embraced by a feeding darkness that snarled with blood-wet teeth. Foam flying from his flanks, my horse tried to outrun his own shadow.

The moon went down before the beast beneath me slowed to a walk, nuzzled in the trickle of water by a rock. Hand to my side, I half-slid, half-fell to the ground. The horse mounted the bank in a shower of clods, snorted, and was gone.

There was a distant howling—wolves, or feral dogs.

All that fog-shrouded night I writhed, gripped by a cold burning. I saw fell things in every patch of darkness, but when the pain eased I slept, tired beyond fear.

I awoke, unable to move, staring at the red dawn sky. Gore crows came, sat watching. One thumped to the ground beside my head. I felt its feathers stir my hair, waited for it to dip its beak in my unblinking eye. One by one the carrion eaters pecked me painlessly, here, there, flew away hungry.

Living things do not feast on the flesh of the undead.

I could not rot, but my unrenewed body frayed as rain and wind had their way with me. When the rain made tears in my hollow sockets I wept with rage. Bad luck to have been the first into conjurer's presence. Better luck that he had never finished speaking.

Dead men do neither good nor ill.

A passing fox clicked sharp teeth on my skull, hungry for the field mouse hiding within. Yellow leaves fell and covered my bare bones. A bellowing stag's hoof crushed a dozen finger joints, burrowing beetles scattered others. I dozed beneath a blanket of snow.

It was summer again, golden twilight. Puffing with effort, a round-faced boy climbed over the lip of the dell. He drank at the spring, ate a great slab of bread with cheese. Hidden in fern-shadow, I watched moonlit mice steal his breakfast while he slept.

The level rays of the rising sun shone on the spare curves of my cheeks when the boy's eyes opened. Eyes on the naked grin of my teeth, he backed away, his breath harsh in the silence. He scrambled up the bank, going back the way he had come.

I, a duke's man, had become a scarecrow for wayward children.

Icicles and new shoots, blossoms, fruit, and fallen leaves. I dreamed of old victories and warrior kings, woke to the heavy chink of harness, the squeak of leather on leather. The iron tang of anger filled my bony nostrils. Caught in the moonlight, the mounted horseman's mouth was a thin line of temper and will.

He backed the horse into the leafy cave beneath the willow, drew his sword in a whisper of sharp metal. The moon sank, the sun rose, the insect drone grew louder with the heat of the day: he and his steed were one statue. Only the light ran up and down his blade a little as they breathed.

A hunter must have patience.

I heard them long before he did, although his ears were keen and the horse's keener. They clambered over the rim of the dell, eager for spring water and shade. Farmers, ignorant of the arts of war, deserting to do their first plowing. Churls, hardly worth a soldier's attention.

But he was no warrior.

There was a flash of light that had nothing to do with sunshine on steel. The peasants stood paralyzed. Their eyes glittered with terror as, one by one, the horseman carved their hearts out, spoke words of power, and sent the corpses marching back to his army.

You cannot kill the dead.

Meaning to wipe his blade, the spell-shaper backed his horse into the ferns. Under the leaf-mould sticks and bones cracked. The animal stumbled as my skull rolled and was crushed under a hind hoof. In a jangle of harness, the rider fell. Reins trailing, the beast hobbled away on three legs.

The naked sword had been driven entirely through the man.

One hand to his wound, the spell-shaper raked the leaves with his free fingers, grinned bitterly when he saw my splintered cranium. "No living man—can defeat—me." Blood drooled from his mouth.

His fingers curled around the sword's hilt. A ripple of brilliance ran down the blade, but nothing more. His eyes rolled, refocussed, and he reached out and gripped. Hand on a fragment of my skull he knew me for one of the undead.

And I knew he would have to end my bane to save himself.

His brows knotted with effort, the dying man's blood-slick fingers tightened. I willed myself to slip from his hand. Ferns rustled, a cloud-shadow slid across the grass, somewhere a hare thumped and was still—

I yielded.

"Be as you once were," he whispered. Hollow bone reshaped itself beneath his hand. "Be as you once were." I felt my jaws clatter together, my teeth seek their sockets. "Be as you once were." My neck bones wriggled among the leaves, crawled on the ground, seeking the burden of my cranium—

Something broke in him. He died, snarling at the pain.

All day long the flies buzzed, busy at their feeding. The gore crows came, and the fox lurked, waiting for the birds to leave for the night. The field mouse stayed frozen with terror in its grass-lined hollow.

All night threads and rags of my flesh crawled to me, joined together. The dead man's spell, slow but sure, not swift enough to save him, nonetheless transformed me. Naked, whole, I woke to a clatter of spears on shields that was only the wind in the trees. I wrapped myself in the corpse's cloak and came away, leaving him to my wild companions.

I live on the charity of strangers, lady. If the story pleased you, a bite of bread would be welcome. A cup of milk if you can spare it. A man gets hungry when his bones wear flesh.

The Hungry Season

The hunter had killed two deer close together, and was bundling the meat in the hides to drag to his canoe hidden on the riverbank, when he smelled a foul odor on the wind, although it was frozen winter.

He was prepared to sacrifice one deer to wolves, but what watched him might be smarter and more dangerous than a pack in the hungry season. Nonetheless he called out in a friendly fashion, "There is plenty of meat."

An old man in ragged doeskin walked out of the trees and stopped.

"There is plenty here," called the hunter. "Come, we will roast the hearts and become stronger." It was usual to eat the liver, but his father, who seldom hunted anymore, was very fond of liver and the hunter had saved those.

The man drew closer. He was battered by the cold and painfully thin but not so old as he seemed at first look. He hobbled as if a toe or two were frostbitten. His hood hid his face.

"There may be wolves about. I will move some way from the butchering place and start a fire," announced the hunter, and walked off, pulling his load. The skins, hair side down, slide easily across the snow.

He could hear the crunch of footsteps as the other followed him, fast for a man as weak as this one looked. The hunter was glad his back trail had been covered by snow. It would be harder to follow it if he lost this contest—if it was a contest.

The other walked steadily, although he lurched from side to side. It might be what it looked like and no more, but the hunter's hands almost shook as coaxed a fire from the dry wood taken from a nearby windfall. Two winters ago his older brother had not come back from hunting, and that had not been as bitter a winter as this one.

The hunter built the little blaze out into a line, the better to roast the two hearts, and the better to keep fire between him and the other. "A big storm coming," he said conversationally, it not being polite to ask for information. "We will need all the firewood we can gather."

The other's dark, thin hands broke sticks and its eyes in their dark pits watched the hunter whenever the hunter was not watching him. It was not venison the other craved, although the meat was roasting, and the smell was inviting.

When the wind blew the wrong way, the stench of what shared the fire was sickening. The hunter knew it must be stronger and swifter than any man who hunts deer, especially ones mysteriously fat and placid in the depths of winter.

That had been a sign this was a dangerous place. His village was hungry or he would have gone on, leaving the deer here alone. Ravening wolves avoided what sat across from him.

The hunter now knew he had not feared it as much as he should have. The smell of death was on it but it was strong, strong enough to break branches with ease.

It built a pile of firewood and the man realized it was playing with him. Each branch was thicker than the last, and all broke with a crack like breaking bone. Putting fear from him, the hunter said, "Thank you. We will be warm and eat well."

"Yes," hissed the creature. There were strings of saliva hanging from the corners of its mouth. Effortlessly, it wrung a thick branch so the wood shattered rather than breaking. "Yes," it said and its drool ran faster.

The hunter drew his knife and tested the meat. It was done. He sharpened a stick, cut a bit, and offered it to his guest. As it took the stick the firelight showed its hand and sleeve clearly. It sat, eyes on the hunter's face.

"It's ready," the hunter said, "and the day is growing cold. Eat, brother."

It looked at him, reflected flames brightening its eyes. "How did you know me?" it asked.

"Our mother made that coat," replied the hunter. "You were wearing it the winter you never came home."

"Yes," said the creature thoughtfully, and almost bit the meat. His brother had been fond of venison. Then whatever there had been of his brother was gone, replaced by something that knew only hunger, but not for deer-flesh.

"Eat, brother," the hunter said again, as if he had not seen the change. He sharpened his own stick and reached to cut venison, seeing his own hand, strong and whole, in the firelight.

The creature watched and its saliva ran. The windigo eats any human being it can, unless it needs a fresh body. His brother was worse than dead and the hunter might be the same soon, for in the light and warmth of the fire it was easy to see the other was battered flesh hanging on blackened bone.

The hunter was the strongest of the young men of the village. "Cross the fire and come to me," he said, opening his furs so the creature could better see the smooth skin lying over hard muscle and smell the man-flesh. "Cross the fire and come to me," he said again. "Cross the fire—"

It leaped at him.

Up went both the hunter's hands, one with his knife and the other with his sharpened stick. He sprang to meet the windigo and stabbed it in both its eyes. Blinded, it roared and reached again. If it could no longer see the hunter, it could smell him, and it needed a new body more than ever.

The hunter drove the stick, deep, deeper, and slashed with the knife at the creature's scalp, neck, face. Scarlet threads and beads of blood steamed on the snow, and then the windigo jerked and was still: dead, perhaps, or perhaps not.

The hunter heaved all the firewood into the fire, knocking

61

the two roasted hearts into the blaze. Silently, he begged pardon of the deer. With a long pole, he tipped the burning pile onto the windigo's body. Coming to all fours, the creature roared and then collapsed. Then the woods were silent except for the hungry whisper of the flames. His brother had been clever.

Back and forth the hunter went, until all the dead wood he could move with his puny man-strength was piled, burning the body that had been his brother's. Then he squatted, rubbing his clothes clean with snow, watching the flames, and listening. The rising wind hissed through the trees. Falling sleet hissed in the fire.

It grew darker. Presently he saw an icy heart in the midst of the flames. He felt better for the certain knowledge the creature had been a windigo and worse for knowing the windigo's icy heart must be destroyed or the creature would seek another victim.

He was nearest and he knew the way to where his people were waiting: human flesh that would draw a windigo's cannibal lust. His stomach knotted at the thought of eating his father, his mother, his brothers and sisters and cousins. Better he kill himself than that.

The hunter took a burning stick and began scavenging for more wood. The heat was intense enough by now that wet logs would burn, and he rolled some into the flames. It was near full dark when the windigo heart suddenly melted and turned into a drift of steam that floated away toward the river.

The fire raged. The hunter kept watch in the six directions, north, south, east, west, up, and down. When the moon had risen, and the pyre was completely burned out, he dragged his venison to his canoe as fast as he could.

Bundling the meat in, he pushed the canoe out into the water, took his paddle and drove for midstream. As the current took him, he heard something howl and go silent. He looked back and saw what might have been a tree that swayed and moaned in the wind. If so, it swayed and moaned when no other trees did.

There are many things in the forest and those who see them plainly do not come back to tell. Still, it is said that a windigo does not always need a human body. It can wait, cold as ice, big as a tree, wailing like the wind, and hungry for human flesh.

The hunter thrust his paddle deep and sped downstream. Water does not carry a scent and there was hunger in the village. After the feasting would be time enough to tell his father what had happened to his brother. Let the older man decide who needed to know.

Whipped by sleet and snow, he followed the tributary, its shores crusted with ice. All the way, he listened behind him, looked to either side, until finally he felt the swift current of the main river take him and rested his paddle crosswise, ready to use if he needed. The river would take him faster than a man could run, winding through hills too steep to climb.

It was still dark when the hunter grounded his canoe. The crowd of ghostly shapes with hungry stares that came out to see who had arrived suddenly in the night frightened him. Their faces were as hungry as the well-loved face he had seen for one last moment across the fire.

"I have two deer!" he called, "Make ready!" The gaunt ghosts became people he had known all his life hurrying this way and that. He was home and safe, with a tale that would wait to be told. "Father," he called with pride, "there are two livers!"

"You're a good son," the older man said, watching the people, and then, more quietly, "and telling whatever you have seen and done will wait. It would be best if you changed your clothes. You stink of burned flesh." The two men looked at one another. They had both hunted in the forest in the hungry season.

Heaven Shed Tears

My daughter holds a needle threaded with silk between her lips. I touch my little finger to the doubled thread and let a drop of water slid along it so her naked mouth glistens. The sight is obscene. This forbidden ritual is unique to our family, linking generation to generation. My grandmother was labeled an RR, reduced-rights, when she would not explain what it was she was doing when surprised with a cup of water open to the air.

Things never went well for her after that, yet now I sit, back braced against a door, holding the flimsy panel closed, doing as she did. All of our living space is held in common, and no door has a lock other than as the ship's safety requires. I hear feet in the corridor as I let the second drop of water slip down the thread. My hand is steady. Water is too precious to spill. I am old enough that I can afford to be brave.

My daughter blinks. We are staring at one another, although the air is so dry our eyes hurt. Like everyone on board we always wear masked protective suits that recycle our wastes and conserve water. Only during these stolen moments do we see one another's faces, always strange. This year her face is losing its childish roundness and her cheekbones are beginning to show. She is beautiful, with fine-grained skin and perfect teeth. I never was, never wanted to be, in a way.

My face is strong, my hands are strong, and both are scarred. My teeth are marred from malnutrition and bones that should be straight and long are twisted. My generation had to meet many challenges. Born midway in the journey, we never saw Earth and few of us will see our destination, a pair of water-rich planets circling a yellow sun. "We are the link," we say. "The link that makes the chain." The Heavenly Twins, someone named those blue worlds, nothing like the glowing cinder that the ship saw as it left its home solar system. It was then, I think, our forbearers grasped that there would never be any going back, ever, for anyone.

I send the third drop of water on its way. The needle rests in the fold of my daughter's pink, glistening tongue. On Earth, children caught rain-drops and snowflakes open-mouthed, water fallen from the sky. That's in the remembrance book my grandmother wrote for us. Its slight weight presses against my heart. It is with me always. She made it smaller than the palm of my hand, of things that grew around her or were part of her household.

The cover of our book is silk, heavy and fine, with a bit of braid and a tassel for a bookmark. Both were cut from a gold and red dragon scarf that belonged to my grandmother's grandmother. Grandmother made the paper and ink herself, such things being rare and of uncertain quality by the time she was chosen to embark. She was proud to be one of the crew and yet when I read her book as a child and found it rich with things she left behind I could not imagine how she could leave Earth. Finger poised, I hear voices, not very near, and release the fourth drop of water.

When I grew older, I read the ship's records as we all do, and I knew that world, with its wind, trees, and rain, had died. We didn't know how or why: there was a storm of communications and then nothing but that faint red dot to say: do not come back. Most would not have wanted to but even they, the natural explorers, missed the thought of home at their backs, going on no matter what happened to our ship. From then on, it, with its cargo, might be all that was left.

My world, Generation Ship One, was as dark and as cold as was safe. One by one the scenes that glowed like view screens for our small spaces died. Finally we only used power for the most essential functions and grew skilled at moving in the dark. I was always a little hungry, always a little thirsty. Even now, years after we captured a wandering ball of almost pure ice, drinking all I want is a painful pleasure, for I know the price. People died to bring that water to the ship and among them was my mother. It was her plan and she insisted that she go. The first attempt failed; the second succeeded.

Now we draw near that other sun and the sleeping ship wakes. The power collectors hum as I have never heard them hum before. There are recordings playing everywhere: sounds of the wind and the sea, leaves and grass; pictures of plains and mountains, sunrises and sunsets. There's music, and games, and dancing to do and to watch. The information section is available to anyone for any purpose. There is extra food and it's rumored alcohol is made, although I haven't tasted any. I will when I am offered it. I am hungry for new experiences, although they frighten me.

Someone runs and calls, hidden yet close behind me. A high voice, a child who thinks there are no adults around. This section of the ship was closed until recently, and opened now that there is less need to conserve. I hurry, send the fifth drop of water on its way. My daughter lifts a gloved hand to hold the needle in place as she licks glossy lips. I can remember what it tasted like, that endlessly recycled water exposed to air, foreign to my own body. So strange, that gift of vital fluid, straight from another's reserves.

It's rumored that lovers do it but I've never had a lover. I was a good girl and am a good woman: my life is ruled by charts, tests, and the needs of the expedition as a whole. "We are the link that makes the chain." Therefore I bore this daughter, who is mine and mine alone, since I do not know her father. Indeed, he may not be aboard this ship, but far behind us and long since dust. I learned when I came of age my own father was not one of us and I never asked about hers.

The sixth drop. My eyes, stinging from the dry air, tear. I lick the salt from the corner of my mouth as my daughter curls her lips at my bitter gift. Her eyes brim, too, and not with emotion. If she is like I was, she can hardly wait for this to be over. But she will remember it as better than she thinks it is now. The only memories I have of my mother's face are from just such moments: stolen time.

As I must I send the seventh drop on its way and she accepts it. I hear children in the corridor, calling, running as they should not do and as, being children, they must. I take the threaded needle, weave it back into the cover of the book, hidden among the red, gold, and silver threads. My daughter has already closed her mask. I close mine. In a year or three or six we may see one another again.

For a great deal of my waking life I was angry that I was the instrument of another's will, that my grandmother made this choice for my mother and for me, and for all that may come after. Now I see what they desired. My daughter and I listen and step out into the momentarily deserted corridor. Watching her walk away, through the dappled sunlight projections of long-gone trees, red leaves flying in a wind out of the past, I am proud of her as she is not proud of me. Not yet.

I may or may not reach our goal, but I know sober joy at a job well done. Even though I say nothing now, I can write in the book I carry next to my heart what I feel. "I forged a link in the chain." One day, when the children's children of those who voyaged out of hell stand on alien ground and watch heaven shed tears, I will be one of many who gave their strength so they will taste that rain, the sky's saltless tears.

Summer-Witch

S ummer awoke, as she had awakened many times before, on the broad breast of the hill, the shattered remains of her brown husk around her, and the blue sky overhead. Her legs pointed down the hill, to the south, to the sun. She sat up.

To her left was the open grave of the spring-warlock, his head to the top of their hill, his legs to the east. To her right lay the grass-grown mound of their brother, the autumn-warlock of this domain. The fourth mound—that of their winter-witch, the sister whom Summer never saw—completed their circle of four.

Summer climbed out of her grave, stood tall, arms raised to the sky, stretching. Then she knelt and placed her hands on either side of Spring's sleeping face. *So old*, she thought, feeling the rough skin. Her brother's leaf-green eyes opened. He murmured, "Next year, my sister," and slipped back into dream.

All was well with him, then.

Summer swept the loose earth into his grave, patted it firmly into place, then sat back on her heels, and sighed. Some years the two of them were awake together during season-change. This would be a solitary year, for by the time her autumn brother awoke, she herself would be longing for the sheltering earth and the sleep of seasons.

Summer stood tall, and surveyed her domain.

Further south, other summer-witches had already awakened, and their rich green holdings rolled away to the hazy horizon, beyond which there were farms, villages, towns, and cities—places where the older ways had been bent to new purposes. Farther north, where the spring warlocks had barely had time to bury their winter sisters, the hills were still dun and drear.

When she came here again the northern hills would be red and orange with autumn, and the southern would be turning gold. By then her feet must have pressed every patch of soil, splashed through every stream; her hands must have caressed every plant, patted every animal. Feet drumming on the earth, the summer-witch began the long, sunwise spiral out from the heart-hill of her domain.

It had been foggy and the grassy slopes were slippery. *That was why I fell*, she thought, though she had never fallen before. It was not that many sun-turns since she had found this place and claimed it for her kin and herself. She was not old, not yet.

Hair hanging in strings before her face, Summer lay, tasting earth in her mouth. She was resting just a moment, listening to the roar of the brook at the foot of the hill, gathering strength. The wind shushed through the leaves, splattered her with larger drops.

It was going to rain hard.

One ankle was swelling, yet she must rise. If she did not dance, Autumn would stir in his sleep on the hill, rise early, try save the domain for their four. It was not even halfway through her season. Her brother would be weak, his renewal incomplete. He would fail. They would all die.

Summer staggered up.

Uphill was hard, but she topped the ridge, found a stick and moved carefully downhill, heading for the creek that flowed along the valley. Entering and leaving the water, the stream would carry her presence along its length, enable her to keep the domain's balance with the least possible effort.

Wind shook the groaning trees.

A big storm was gathering fast.

Water splashing about her feet, Summer danced as

strongly as she could. The weakest summer-witch would have the coming turmoil deflected onto her domain by the others. It might take years before a major storm's damage would heal, and their four would be vulnerable while it did.

There were worse fates than simple death.

On her way north, so long ago, Summer had seen gale-stripped woods black and dripping with rot, ground erupting in foul masses of corruption, a danger to every youngling that passed. One such had come at her, eyeless, fingerless, grasping, seeking her life-force to save itself and its kin.

The dying do not show mercy.

A wind-borne branch battered past her, lashed her with wet green leaves. Summer danced on, pain like lightening in her ankle. Through the screen of thrashing foliage, she could see a funnel, twisting about, seeking where it would strike. "Ahh, ahaaa," the summer-witch screamed, driving her terror out from within herself to ward it off.

"Oooooh," it breathed, and struck.

Summer woke, chest pierced through by a jagged branch, groaned, pulled herself free, and fell senseless. Conscious again, she lay listening to her breath bubble and whistle, then rolled over and crawled downhill on hands and knees.

Not dead yet, she thought.

A bedraggled bird crouched on a rock at the edge of the creek. Summer reached out, touched him, watched it flutter up the bank and into the dripping underbrush. Her power was still with her.

If she could dance, she could heal herself.

Summer swayed, got to her feet, trying to establish a rhythm. If she made it to the outer boundary, she could restore her strength on midsummer's day. Striding on her knees, crawling on all fours, dragging herself forward by her fingers when she must, Summer spiraled outward.

No youngling could seize the domain while the four of them lived.

The rap and clatter of hail filled the dark around her. Freak weather, which made Winter stir in her sleep, set the trees to shivering. Teeth locked on her lip, Summer stood still, listened.

"Oo, oo, oo, oo!" fluted something much too near.

A youngling, quest-calling.

A branch rolled under her foot, Summer slipped, fell into an explosion of pain. She thought, I could just quit. Just stop. The others would never know. Endings are as natural as beginnings.

"Oo, oo, oo," sang the voice, full of youth and longing, almost within reach.

Summer looked up into the determined yet callow face, and knew they both thought of her death. Eyes hard, they measured one another. The old summer-witch shifted a leg to ease the pain, and waited for the other to charge.

She was from near the edge of the cities where her kin had reared their pods for generations uncounted, shaping once-sterile earth and sky to the needs of creators so long-lost in the deeps of time they might be only legends.

Awakened to find she was surplus young, she had raced north ahead of the rest of her birth-cadre, seeking an undefended territory. Most who left the shelter of city edges died. Only the strong and lucky survived.

Summer could remember the first time she had come down the valley into this domain, her feet feeling the harsh, cold grass, her hair splattered with sunshine where the trees had not yet woven their canopy of leaves, hoping in every fiber of herself that this might be the place.

The old summer-witch had been on the top of the heart-hill, nothing but a woody skeleton with grass thrusting up through the slats of the ribcage. The elder must barely have made it from her grave before she died, face burned from the sun, flesh crumbling into earth.

Summer had spiked the remaining three of the old four with green, leafy branches. The stakes went in so easily that she wondered if the ancients had not already died in their mounds. She had feared the need to kill, was relieved it was done, that she had felt nothing.

How she had danced to claim her domain! Once, twice, three times over every patch of ground, fingers caressing feathers, fur, hard chitin, scaly skin. When Autumn and Spring had carried the husk of their Winter north, she had been here, ready. None of them mentioned their wonder that she had succeeded where almost all of the cadre would have failed.

Summer had always been the strongest.

The younglings will have to pass me by, she thought. This year at least, I will not be a pale corpse in my green wood. Pain sweeping through her like fire, the summer-witch moved, insensible to anything but the need to survive.

Neck broken by a single blow, the charging youngling crumpled like a rotten branch and was as sweet in her mouth as fresh green twigs. The youngster had been foolish. Old, and wounded, Summer still knew a trick or three.

The sun stood high in the sky when she came to the boundary. With no time to spare, Summer sat, back against a tree, started to spin her thread of power. All through the longest day the summer-witches strove to bind the land in a protective net of force and she worked with them, substituting skill for strength, until she, too, was strong.

All through the short night that followed, Summer lay,

eyes watching the circling of the stars as the land beneath her renewed her. When the sun turned the east rose and gold, the summer-witch began the long, anti-sunward spiral inward, the slow dance that begins the closing of the year.

When the day was no longer than the night, she came, feet drumming on the heart of her domain, up the hill, to kneel and open the autumn warlock's mound. Fingers cut by the fibers of his husk, she pressed her bleeding hand to his smooth forehead. He stirred, looked in her face.

Summer said, "You must wake and I must sleep."

"Yes," said the warlock.

Already her own husk was growing up Summer's neck. Soon it would close her lips, eyes, ears. Autumn took the summer-witch by her rough, thickening arm, lead her to her place. With quick strokes of his unmarked hands, he opened the turf so she could lie within.

She stretched out, feeling the healing earth surround her, closed her eyes as her brother closed her grave, sighed once, and slept again the sleep of seasons. Above her the wind lifted the first yellow leaves into a pale blue sky, blowing them away like forgotten years.

Terra Incognita

I thumped the last box of books and papers onto the table next to the sagging grocery sack full of clementines and avocados, then I pulled up the hem of my t-shirt and wiped my gritty face. It was hot, the end of a long, sticky summer. I was sodden with sweat.

With this box in, I was, finally, officially, moved. I shoved the sagging cardboard a few inches further from falling to the tiles, and sat down, heavily.

I was alone in my own place.

Having tried a nuzzle in the stuffy darkness of the stairway and found I was about as interested in him as the newel post was, George had excused himself and gone on his way, looking for better company for a Saturday night.

I didn't grudge him — I was exhausted.

I sat down, spraddled my legs to the cooling breeze from the oscillating fan. Besides the fruit, there was hamburger, rolls, and a deli carton of macaroni salad in the sack. I'd meant to fix both of us dinner, but I hadn't been sorry when George said he'd leave me to settle in. He'd lingered just long enough that I could have said, no, stay, if I'd wanted to.

I scratched the sweat-prickle at my waistband. Good old George. How grateful I'd felt as I listened to the departing pad of his sneakers on the stairs. I liked him. I liked it better that he had the sense to quit when he was ahead. I'd had a hard day packing before he'd shown up to carry things to his car, and ferry me across town. Good old reliable George.

I fished around inside the rustling sack, pulled out a clementine and began peeling back the skin. I ripped the sections apart. Awkward with hunger, I crammed my mouth with sweetness. Juice ran down my chin.

I jumped at a cold, fluttering touch, but it was only that my left foot had quivered against the metal chair leg. It had been a hard day. Both my legs trembled. I could go on for a long time if I didn't stop, but I was going to be stiff if I sat.

I licked my fingers, wiped them on my shorts, and got up. I began moving around the kitchen, running the water in the sink, plugging the drain with the pink rubber flap. I took my drooping houseplants from their box and put them into a lukewarm inch or so of water. I could almost hear them sigh with relief.

I lifted the dank hair at the back of my neck, and looked around, figuring how many tasks I could get away with skipping before I went to sleep. I thought, *I'd better make the bed right now—*

Never mind that I'd clearly marked the one box I wanted in bold red and carried it in first myself, it took me a good while to find it. I'd packed the stuff I'd need immediately— sheets, towels, soap, shampoo, a clean, pressed pair of jeans, even two brand-new t-shirts in their logoed plastic bags. And a wad of clean, wrinkled laundry I'd never had time to fold.

When I stopped trying to remember where I'd put the box and started searching systematically, I tripped over it almost immediately, hidden behind a barricade of later arrivals George had carried in.

I wrestled the rough-dried whiteness onto the unfamiliar bed, sacked the pillows in the cases, pulled the top sheet into place, tucked it in at the foot, tight, hospital style, and turned one corner down. I was almost unwilling to touch anything, it all looked so clean and I felt so dirty.

I put the towels, soap and other toiletries in the bathroom, averting my eyes from the long rust stains in the sink and tub. Tomorrow for them. Or the day after. It'd be a shower tonight.

I left the clothes in a stack on the upper shelf of the closet. Whoever had cleaned the place out hadn't left a single wire coat hanger.

I went back into the sunny kitchen and packed the spoilables into the stale-smelling refrigerator, first fingering the sweaty carton of macaroni to be sure it was still cold. Then I took another clementine and peeled it in a long, slow ribbon, enjoying the sharp, orange tang.

I slipped the rind on my left wrist. It made a broad armlet spiraling almost to my elbow. I bit into the sections, one by one, feeling the tense skin part under my teeth, the crushed pulp spurt onto my tongue.

I used the penknife from my purse to halve, then quarter, an avocado. God knows where the box with the kitchen stuff had gotten to, and I was famished. I laid the stone on the drain board to dry after I pried it free. Avocados make good houseplants. I already had two.

I peeled a third clementine, picking the sections meticulously clean and making a little pile of white threads in one hollow avocado skin. The second spiral made a bracelet for my right arm. They stained my wrists and forearms yellow with their oil. I lifted my arm and sniffed the fragrance of orange and sweat, oddly enticing.

I alternated bites of what remained of the avocado with sections of orange.

Mouth full, I closed my eyes to enjoy the contrast of taste and texture. The chartreuse meat was too firm to yield to the pressure of my tongue, too soft to offer any resistance to my teeth. The sweet-sour clementine juice complimented the suave richness—

I sank my teeth into the fruits and imagined stalking through the jungle. A savage hunter decorated with the hides of her victims, I scrabbled through leafy thickets, following the citrus tang, the oily musk—

I'd been staring through the forest of houseplants in the sink at the still-sunny street for several minutes without really seeing anything, when the brappp of a passing motorcycle broke my reverie. I was practically asleep where I sat.

I wasn't going to get any more done tonight. I wiped my

hands on my dingy shirt—the paper towels were in the kitchen box—then massed the golden globes and purple-green pear-shapes together in the corner of the counter. They'd look good on the living room window ledge. I'd find my brass fruit bowl tomorrow.

I folded the empty grocery sack flat with fussy care. I told myself I was saving it for tomorrow's garbage, but the truth was I had so few things out of the boxes that every usable item that helped fill the bare space seemed precious.

I gathered the green and orange scraps of fruit peel in one hand, opened the sagging screen door, and went down the steps at the back, bare feet wincing at the sun-baked bricks. The walk was in the shade now, but it held the day's heat. I was looking for the trashcans. I found the white-painted garbage enclosure was at the rear of the lot, next to the alley.

I lifted the white wooden cover and gagged.

Although they were clean and plastic-lined, after days in the sun the cans stank. I got the lid up and the rinds in as fast as possible, pressed the yielding plastic lid firmly home again. I re-snapped the bungee-cord someone had added as extra protection against strays, wondering if it was coons, dogs, or cats they worried about.

Or foxes. They came into town, too.

I turned around to face a stick-thin old woman with a folded-over lunch sack that must have been the orts from her own dinner. She ran disapproving eyes up and down my long, bare legs, the orange peels on my arms, the sweaty straggle of my hair. "Mrs. Rusling wants all trash wrapped."

Although most of the garbage in the can *had* been wrapped in grease-darkened paper bags, I wasn't the only sinner. In one brief, breath-holding glimpse, I'd seen a tangle of nibbled crusts of freezer pizza, a weary half-head of lettuce, and a clutch of deflated tomatoes oozing seeds down the liner.

"I didn't know," I said.

Mrs. Busybody waited, plainly expecting I was going to

turn around and fish amid the stinking relics.

I didn't.

The narrow mouth grew a little tighter. "You're in Mrs. Taylor's place," she said. It wasn't quite an accusation.

"Apartment 2," I said briskly, stepping off the walk to get around her.

"Mrs. Rusling doesn't want us walking on the grass."

I stepped back onto the hot bricks, mission accomplished. I wasn't the only one to ignore that edict either. Most of the yard was hard-trodden earth, clearly showing the paths to the tool shed, around to the front. Where there was grass, it was nothing more than unmown hay.

"Lorna's place," she said.

What could I say? Lorna must have been Mrs. Taylor.

I started back up the walk, too angry to introduce myself, wishing I hadn't met her. I was suddenly absolutely certain that she'd waited, peeking from behind her drapes, to bring her garbage out.

She'd probably been disappointed when George left. Now she'd have to wait to find out if he was my boyfriend or my brother or just hired help. *Poor* thing. I hoped she had a restless night of it.

The level rays of the setting sun cast my gigantic shadow on the house. If I'd been alone, I'd have raised my arms and crooked my fingers, made a fierce face, and growled to myself. Boogie man gonna get you, yess he iss!

"—be ashamed of yourself," said a whispery voice behind my back, so soft I wasn't quite sure I heard it.

I looked up at the back of the house.

Three big bay windows, and one small one. That was mine. My bedroom.

The nearest large window had brown and white striped drapes and beige sheers that moved as I looked, flick, flick. Someone had stepped away to avoid being seen.

The middle one had its center panel up a few inches, its scalloped and fringed shade swinging slowly in and out in the moving air. Whoever was there was smart enough to stay still, but that strip of dainty flowered print had to be a dress, not a slipcover.

The farthest window was filled with a moon-faced figure that didn't bother to move. Mrs. Rusling, I thought, although I couldn't be sure. I'd rented from an agent.

What had I done to deserve three meddlesome old witches for neighbors?

I shrugged, let the screen swing to behind me with a flat whack that might be taken as a comment.

I'd moved *here*, that's what. The neighborhood was an old one that was reluctantly getting younger as its original residents died out. I'd picked this house because it was in a good location, and was well-kept and affordable.

I wasn't expecting to make friends with any of my neighbors. The three or four people of my own age I'd passed while going and coming from the bus stop a block away had studiously ignored me and I, them.

If I'd wanted ready-made pals I'd have moved to a big apartment block at the foot of Coss's Hill or out on Pecos Way, where everybody was everybody's buddy, and arguments about enforcing the house rules against beer bottles on the pool patio filled the commercial breaks in the cabled-in sports.

Not my kind of crowd, not that any crowd was. I had my own friends—and good old George.

I could bear the three witches.

Back in the house, I toured around, making sure all the unfamiliar windows were closed, the front door's bolts thrown home. The glassy stare of the uncurtained bay window in the living room repelled me, so I dragged down the dusty-smelling shades and left the former parlor to melancholy twilight, closing the rumbling double doors behind me.

My bathroom and bedroom were off the kitchen—small close rooms, meant for the maid or the cook originally. I

wouldn't have to go back into my living room until morning.
By tomorrow evening I've have unpacked lamps, and done
something for drapes so I wouldn't put on a shadow-play for
every passing stranger, but for tonight the parlor was
abandoned territory.

My kitchen had been the dining room, before the door
was cut through to the servant's quarters. My plebeian little
sink, stove, and refrigerator huddled awkwardly together in
one corner where it had been convenient to pull the electric
and gas lines through. They were an insult to the stately
proportions of the place.

I didn't mind. Most of the room was untouched, golden
with the last sunlight, elegant even in its old age. The broad
window ledge, now cruddy with paint, had probably once
been a cushioned seat, made private by two or three layers of
drapes. I sat down, imagining the heavy velvet, the cobweb
lace, the swaged valance, the close smell of furniture polish
and old potpourri.

The setting sun gilded the late summer olive of the
scraggly plane trees into near-medieval beauty. This was
going to be the perfect spot to sit and read, waiting for the
microwave to beep. I could just take a moment to enjoy my
good fortune before I got back to work.

I went to the table and pawed through the sagging carton,
wanting to try it out immediately. It mostly things I'd nearly
thrown out and then decided not to discard at the last minute,
when I was too tired to make any more decisions.

There were seven or eight paperbacks with their covers
worn dim and flaky. One or two glossy magazines there
hadn't been time to read this month. Yesterday's newspaper.

I'd tossed my last handful of mail on top, too. Bills, in
their windowed envelopes. A half-dozen flyers. A postcard
from a vacationing friend that I flicked with annoyance. I
wasn't vacationing this year. I was moving.

There was nothing I wanted to look at now.

I reached deeper, fingers clawing through musty

newsprint—

The wire coil of the old spiral notebook pricked my thumb. I hauled it out, sorry all over again that I hadn't trashed it. I was sorry every time I noticed it, but I was never able to get rid of it. My sister and I had made it seven—no, now it was eight—summers ago.

Before she died.

I ran a hand over the wallpaper wrapped and pasted over its cardboard covers. This had been a bit from the extra roll for the master bedroom, so much prettier than the bouquets of daisies scattered over our own walls. We'd sneaked it out of the basement, careful to cut it as it had been cut by the paper hanger, sneaked it back a foot shorter than it had been.

The endless fall of white roses and green leaves on celadon was splotched brown in one place. A couple of years ago, I'd dropped a teabag on it before rescuing it from the meat wrappings and carrot peels in my kitchen trash.

I slapped the book down on the counter as if the scratched white Formica was Ted's foolish, near-handsome face. I was sorry I'd never told him how much I hated him. He'd died two years ago, drunk at the wheel again. That time he'd been alone.

With only a year's difference in age, my sister and I were both drawn and pressured together. We shared one of the three bedrooms in the old clapboard house my grandfather had helped build. My parents had one, and the other, "the guest room," was reserved for the boy they hoped might yet come. A large room with a niche for the bed and a double closet, it was a forbidden wasteland of pink baby things waiting to be refurbished blue.

The two of us traded clothes and hairbrushes, homework and secrets. Hated and fought, too, of course. This notebook was the chronicle of our joint kingdom. Shalalire in Eft. My lips moved silently in the long-unspoken syllables. I opened the cover, tilted the pages to the evening light.

The inside cover was a map, painstakingly drawn in

colored pencils, of the island continent of Eft. I could remember the skittering pressure I applied to the pencil to create that crenelated coastline, as nervously irregular as any real shore, each indentation having its own indentations and so on down to the invisible tremors of my hand so long ago.

The Mountains of Morren ran in long hump-backed lines along the eastern edge of Eft, looping around to protect our kingdom, Shalalire, from everywhere but the sea. To the west were the Seven Cities and the Three Kingdoms, each designated by my minuscule lettering, blurred with time and handling.

The entire northwest corner was rough and scrubby, empty except for the block capitals in my sister's hand. TERRA INCOGNITA she'd printed. We'd never agreed on what should be there, and she'd had erased my drawing—

I pressed my hand to the page as if covering unseemly nakedness.

My eyes teared.

Bastard.

Ted had run his car off the road and into a tree, out of sight in the bushes in the darkness. The State Police told his family that he died instantly. The rumor around town was that he'd tried to get out, and eventually bled to death, too drunk to free himself. Sometimes I hoped that was true.

My sister hadn't died instantly. There had been long days of waiting in the hospital, watching Joanna jerk and writhe in meaningless motions, fighting the straps that held her safe in the high-sided bed that looked like a crib.

Everyone said how brave I was to stay with her.

I kept my guilty secret. I haunted my sister's hospital room because I wanted to be the first one she saw when she woke. An undying princess of Shalalire, she would sleep and wake released from the evil enchantment of the false prince—

Fifteen, I was far too old to believe such stuff, and yet I *did* believe all through the long summer days Joanna lay dying.

Every night I crouched by our window, and I tried to weave our imaginary magic. Chronicles open on the sill before me, I murmured invocations we'd written together, spilled a propitiatory drop or two of her cologne onto the window sill—

The notebook slipped in my hands. I grabbed, and then let it go to avoid tearing the fluttering pages. The corners had been worn round long ago. Another fall would do it no harm at all. It flopped onto the dusty floor and lay face down.

I bent and pulled it back into my lap.

The moon had waxed and waned while, strung with tubes and wires, my beautiful sister slowly wasted into something grotesquely inhuman. Toward the end, my father would only come to stand in the door once a day for a few moments, and my mother refused to come at all. "I want to remember her as she was," she said, and Dr. Freiberg nodded in understanding.

It was summer vacation, and without Joanna I didn't know what to do with myself. The hospital staff was kind, letting me keep all sorts of strange hours. I knew they thought there was no hope, but they were wrong. I *knew* they were wrong.

After one of the nurses told me the sense of hearing remained even for the unconscious, I sat and talked to Joanna for hours, describing the changing shapes of clouds, the passage of sunlight across the brown-tiled floor. What I'd seen on the way to the hospital. What we'd had for dinner. What we'd had for breakfast. Anything, so she knew she wasn't alone.

I was afraid to whisper about Eft, about Shalalire. The hospital personnel whisked in and out unexpectedly, fitting Joanna's care into the pauses between more urgent cases. I wouldn't risk breaking our vow of absolute secrecy by one of them overhearing. It might spoil the magic I made every night.

Day after day, while the hot sun of summer rode up and down the cloudless sky and the respirator huffed and chuffed,

I whispered to her, willing her to hear me, to heal.

One quiet summer afternoon she died.

I think it happened while I was there, although the endless mechanical sigh went on and on without a change. Her face relaxed, and her knotted hands fell open, as if releasing their grip on life—

That was exactly what I thought as I watched, "releasing their grip on life." I stood up, wondering if I should call someone, then was ashamed, thinking I was dramatizing what was probably some perfectly ordinary thing, like the vague smile Joanna sometimes gave the empty air.

A nurse came in, looked at what was on the bed, tidied the cover in the usual way, and told me it was time to go home. I began to argue—it was early, I'd stayed later before, often, Joanna might think I'd tired, abandoned her. She shooed me out with remorseless pleasantness, said there were things they needed to do for my sister.

I hadn't been home ten minutes when the phone rang, and my mother's histrionic wail ended the silence that had filled our house for weeks. Joanna was dead.

I didn't cry. Not then.

Ted came to the funeral, sat there in the back of the church as if *he* had a right to mourn her. I knew where he was by the stir of heads, looking back, ever so casually, one by one. I could feel him there, as if he let off heat. Or sucked the light out of the air.

I hated him. All through the service, I hated him so hard that his skin should have smoked and charred, his hair burst into stinking flame. I wouldn't look back until I smelled the burning, saw the others turn to stare—

Nothing happened of course. Under the prod of my mother's hand in my back, I even managed to thank him for coming as we came down the steps to the train of cars waiting behind the white hearse. I was very polite. I was amazed how polite I was, as though I were shaking with grief, not rage.

All I wanted was to sink my fingernails into his face, to peel the mask of skin off the smooth-shaved cheeks, break the straight nose, smash the even teeth his dentist had already repaired. Show everyone the monster lurking there.

I sat on the hot leather seat, surrounded by the sick scent of too many flowers, and hated so hard I had the whole car to myself. There were plenty of others for the rest of them. Plenty of everything.

Everything was nice for the funeral. People remarked on it particularly. Everything was so nice for Joanna. My mother, old-fashioned proper in her well-fitted black dress and scrap of a hat, had been preparing for weeks. I hated *her* for that, that she'd had time to think of hats and clothes, of flowers and burial plots and perpetual care.

Even the disgusting pink granite headstone was ready. Joanna loathed pink. So did I.

When we got to the cemetery, I could see the grave had been open for days, its piled dust held in place by a tarp. The hole itself had been protected by another tarpaulin that had been pulled onto the first so that the undertaker's men could arrange a fan of branches to cover the opening.

The coffin dropped through the leaves and vanished like a conjurer's trick. Now Joanna is in her grave, I thought, her final resting place. I thought the words again. They meant nothing.

We left before more than the token handful or two of soil had been tossed in, clattering on the casket. My car passed the yellow backhoe that would do the real work on the way out, and I looked hate at it, too. It rumbled by, as uncaring as everything else.

As the days passed, I found that Joanna's death almost didn't matter to me. I'd spent so much time talking to her that I went right on doing it. Knowing her motionless, shrunken form was moldering in the satin-padded white coffin in Evergreen Glades cemetery made no difference.

For the rest of the summer and the first weeks of school,

Joanna lived inside my head, went everywhere with me, talked to me constantly. I had to be careful: the one time I referred to Joanna as if she were alive my mother screamed at me that I was a cold, cruel child to forget. A monster—

Father shushed her quiet.

My hands knotted on the notebook. I'd thought she'd be with me forever, but Joanna-in-my-head had faded away as the months passed, until finally there were whole days and nights when I didn't notice that she wasn't there.

In the end I hadn't even had grief to keep me company.

I went to school, to college, found a suitable job in computers—"a hot field" Ted would have said—and my life went on just as if I'd never had and never lost a sister.

I smoothed the crumpled paper, pressed my hand against the map, as if I could see the square-shouldered letters, "TERRA INCOGNITA," through my palm. I lifted the first page and let it flutter back, unread.

The sunlit street beyond the kitchen window blurred.

I remembered Joanna, brown hair brushing the pages as she wrote, carefully ruling the double-bordered squares for me to fill with decorative capitals. I'd argued that I should do the drawings first, and then she should print the text, but in the end we did it her way — Joanna was the older, after all.

I didn't have to open the notebook to know what the first capital looked like. It was an "I," a column of carefully drawn blocks of stone crowned by a prancing stag whose branching antlers bore green leaves.

"It *was* in golden Shalalire, city of the sun, on the first day of summer, when Asdact ordered the carving of the Head of Jade. Mardant Fromalon was greatly offended that the statue was of the god of the Asharals, and not of the Kenalt—"

Joanna always insisted on the emphasis on the "was."

I stared into nothing, trying to hear more of her voice. I only came to myself when I shuddered all over with the fading adrenaline reaction from my anger. The notebook in my hands closed thoughtlessly, a small clap in the stillness.

I hadn't read the chronicles since Joanna died.

It was my mother who brought them to me. She'd been separating our things, preparing to give away whatever couldn't be made useful for me to the church—the extra bed, the recorder I'd never learned to play, the dolls she said I was too old for—

The minister had come in his mini van to pick up the final boxfuls, to thank her for her gift, and to offer her the formal comfort of religion. She went out to get "one or two things," and I was left alone with him with nothing to say.

I sat, back straight as a ruler, a cup of weak tea in my hands, a dry, store-bought cookie turning to into a sour paste around my teeth, waiting until I could decently get up and go back to mourning my sister in proper silence.

"How are things in school?" asked the minister.

"Fine," I muttered. I hadn't thought about school for months and we were weeks from September's opening day.

He started to say something else and subsided, stirring his tea around and around to pass the time.

I looked into my own cup, watching the fine dust from the tea bag scribble indecipherable patterns at the bottom, then settle into the seam at the foot to form a perfect circle.

When mother came in with the last box, she pulled the notebook out from underneath and thrust it at me. I jumped. I could feel a blood-warm splatter of tea on my hands. When I looked down, the saucer was full, slopping into my lap.

"You'll want it to remember your sister by," she said, her sweet, public smile well in place, although I could see her pleasure in having found our secret. "I know it's painful now, dear, but you shared something very special together."

The minister, seated on the puffy, fashionably camel-backed couch, beamed at this evidence of motherly understanding.

I snatched the notebook from her hands and fled in a consuming rage that didn't prevent me from hearing either the small death of my teacup or my mother's "poor thing," in her most cultivated tones, both followed by a ministerial rumble.

Bitch.

I jammed the notebook home under the bills, pulled the box off the table and thrust it into the corner by the refrigerator, settling it against the wall with a shove from my foot.

Worthless bitch.

Outside, the light had softened into a purple-plum twilight that was swiftly shading into night. I'd have to turn on the harsh, bare overhead bulb in the center of the ceiling if I wanted to stay up. Whoever had stripped the place after the last tenant had taken the covers from the light fixtures, the switch plates, and, I guessed, even the doorknobs, for the ones in place now were green with corrosion and turned stiffly.

The shower gurgled and spat rusty water for two or three minutes before it gave up and went to work. I turned and turned in place beneath the head, watching the water meander clean rivulets down my legs and arms, before I finally soaped up my washcloth and began scrubbing in earnest.

I'd left my filthy clothes in a heap on the floor. Tomorrow I'd find the clothes hamper. I sudsed up my hair, working the thick foam into my scalp, bending my neck to the shower. Again. And a third time.

My two improvised bracelets lay on the edge of the sink, filling the moist bathroom air with the scent of oranges. Lulled by the steady massage of the water I sang, "Oh, my darling, oh my darling, oh my darling Clementine—" over and over, never getting any further in the song, filling my lungs with the steaming air.

I swung the dial completely over. The shock of cool water made me start and goose bump, but I stayed under the stream until I was as near-numb as I was going to get. I was breathless when I stepped out onto the mat. I swayed there for a moment, almost, but not quite, dizzy.

Time to get to bed, I told myself firmly. There was nothing that wouldn't wait for the morning.

The bedroom air was cool only by contrast with the foggy bathroom. If I had felt more at home I would have opened the window to air the place out, although there was little to choose between inside and outside. Indeed, given the neighborhood garbage had been ripening for nearly a week and not everyone was as careful as Mrs. Rusling, the scent of clementines and shampoo was probably far more pleasant than the night air.

Naked, I lay down on the rough top sheet, then grimly made myself get up and pull on clean briefs and t-shirt, laid my shorts and sandals ready to hand, ready for anything.

The other three tenants probably wore frilled caps to bed—or pointed hats. I smiled at my thought. They were just curious old women, and I was just tired.

I woke around midnight to the muffled sounds of the city. The bark of a dog or a fox somewhere far away. The shuss of a passing car, cruising fast now that the streets were almost empty. The rhythmic purr of the fan in the kitchen that I'd not thought to move or turn off.

I lay absorbing the nighttime feel of the unfamiliar room.

To me, one of the most important things about a place is how it feels in the dark, whether it is secure and filled with the pleasant inconsequential noises of a house that has been happily occupied before.

I've never lived in a new house, and I have occasionally wondered what it would be like to be the first to impress your personality on a house, or if you could even do so, given that most people just brought whatever it pleased some builder to put up. I sighed and stared up and the plaster ceiling's fanwise swirls, measure of some-long-dead plasterer's reach.

Deep in the wall, something clicked and settled. I shivered a little, wondering how many people had listened to that small sound in the dark. Generations of quiet nights. On that thought, I fell asleep again.

When I woke a second time I knew I wasn't alone. The air felt different, moving in whispering currents, or too still. Something like that. I held myself motionless, tried to keep my breathing level and smooth.

I was remembering the story of Lee's about one of her friends who had awakened to a man in her room, riffling the contents of her purse.

He must have known by the change in Sandra's breathing that she was awake and terrified. He had bent over her, placed a knife at the point of her jaw, and pushed. A little. Enough to make the knife point break the skin. She'd lain still, shaking with terror, for long minutes while the blood dribbled down her neck. He had stripped her of her valuables with leisurely care, then left as he came, by the fire escape, after wishing her goodnight.

She'd never been able to sleep in the room again.

Sandra had been lucky. She knew it, and, mouths full of salad and sandwich, Lee and I knew it too. "A little white scar, right there—" Lee reached above our lunch plates, smeared with French dressing and catsup, and tapped me on the throat. I'd jumped at her touch and dropped my last bite of grilled cheese on sourdough, threatened by the echo of Sandra's terror.

But Sandra had left a window open on a hot summer night, and I was sure I'd checked everything. I hadn't changed the locks yet, though. Could someone have had a key? God know who, one of the movers? A handyman?

The present crawled by far more slowly than the drops of sweat that formed and skittered down my sides. I counted my breaths. Nice and slow. Nice and slow. My heart pounded so hard I thought I might faint.

I didn't have a phone, even if I should have a chance to use it, and the thick walls of the old house made my neighbors hearing me problematical. Assuming they weren't all deaf as stones anyway.

Could I run fast enough to make it through the door into the street, yell, "Fire!" and wake the neighborhood? I'd sound like a maniac, but I'd be alive.

Something in the kitchen rustled.

I rolled over to look that way before I even thought. On my side, eyes wide open, I could see there was nothing there, nothing in the room with me but the last rays of the setting moon.

But I wasn't alone. I could feel a presence quite distinctly, like a pressure of air on my face, or a fleeting fragrance.

She was surprised.

Apologetic.

Just on her way out.

"Wait," I said aloud, fighting my way out of the knot of sheets, but by the time I freed myself, she was gone. I sat on the edge of the bed, straining to find some unused sense that would let me re-establish contact.

Nothing.

But I knew I'd just met Lorna.

In her courteous flight she had left me with a handful of facts. She had gotten into the habit of wandering around her old place and remembering. She hadn't known anyone was here or she'd not have disturbed me. She did apologize, and I mustn't worry, she wouldn't bother me again. I could almost hear her murmuring oh dear, oh dear as she hurried away to wherever, years late for a final appointment.

Angry and disappointed, as if I'd been brushed off by someone I'd wanted to meet, I stood up. I had a few questions, she could have answered—

I glanced into the bathroom—empty—then went into the kitchen and took a drink from the faucet. My face was brushed by the leaves of the plants I'd left in the sink. I took deep breaths, smelling the damp soil, the scent of green. Then I fumbled my way across the unfamiliar room and opened the parlor doors.

As I expected, that was empty, too. The two heavy chairs

and the sofa stood, backs against the walls as they had for years. A little dust stirred in the draft along the floor.

I stood there, wondering how it had been, where she'd put the end tables, if there'd been knickknack shelves on the walls, and vases of pampas grass in the corners. What they'd done with her keepsake albums and photographs after she—

Died.

I turned around as if someone had tapped my shoulder. I hadn't really thought of her as dead. Discorporate, sure. But not dead-and-buried dead. I sat down in the parlor widow seat, still bewildered. Batted by my elbow, the shade gradually swung itself still. Dust pricked my nose with memories of things I'd never seen.

Ashes to ashes, dust to dust. I looked around the dark room, whose shadows seemed so full of forgotten life, then blinked and bit down hard on my lip, as if someone could see my tears. Had Joanna tried to find *her* things, the things our mother had scattered to the indifferent hands of strangers? Surely she'd look for—

I dumped the box out on the kitchen floor to retrieve the notebook and went back to the blue dimness of the parlor, across dark boards that sighed and shifted under my bare feet. Crouched beside the window seat, one cheek on the grooved woodwork, I willed remembrance, called the unknown and the forgotten. Made magic.

Joanna, laughing, against a patch of blue sky dappled with the spring-green elm leaves.

Joanna, furious, pulling the chronicles from my clenched hands because she didn't like what I'd done.

Joanna, on her side, asleep, while I listened to the vague going-to-bed noises of my parents, waiting to wake her so we both watch moonrise on the first full night of summer.

Joanna dead—

I refused the picture of the shriveled corpse trapped beneath the ground, hugged myself to myself, arms around thighs, and muffled the harsh, ugly sounds of desolate longing with my own flesh. I willed her to come to me, willed her with all my strength. If that old woman could come, why not Joanna? Why not—

I concentrated so hard there was nothing but myself, the pressure of flesh on flesh, the thud of my heart, the taste in my mouth, nothing.

Nothing.

Nothing.

Nothing—

The jolt of pain brought me back. My legs had cramped. Leaning against the wall, feeling the rough plaster against my face, the hard line of the woodwork across my skull, I made my legs unfold. In the kitchen I could hear the fan swing back and forth, back and forth, rhythmic and uncaring, as something, my bills perhaps, or the scattered newspapers, fluttered and slid in its breeze.

Nothing had come. No one had answered.

My dead had stayed dead.

The window shade was lavender with the pale light of the false dawn. I pulled it down a little bit, then let it slide up to show the empty city street, filled with the ambiguous moving shadows of the silhouetted trees. A wind was coming. The heat spell had broken.

I sat down on the dusty ledge, opened to the notebook's first page, took a deep breath, and forced my eyes to Joanna's careful printing. In the pale light of the unrisen sun, I began reading the chronicles of Eft—

"It was in golden Shalalire, city of the sun, on the first day of summer, when Asdact ordered the carving of the Head of Jade. Mardant Fromalon was greatly offended that the statue was of the god of the Asharals, and not of the Kenalt—"

For the last time, I could hear my sister's voice.

When I was done, I went and got the folded grocery sack, slid the battered notebook into it, folded the top down and over so I had a firm, flat package. I pulled on my shorts, side my feet into sandals, and gathered the orange rinds from the bathroom.

I had spent too long with the things of childhood.

It was time to throw them away.

When I'd pressed the book well down into the can, tossed the bracelets in after, closed the lid, snapped the bungee-cord, and lowered the white wood over it all, I stood a moment, feeling for the pain.

Down the alley I could already hear the grind and rattle of the garbage truck. With a spurt of panic, I put my hand on the lid of the can, then, more slowly, pulled it away. No. I didn't want it back. This was going to hurt, but I didn't want it back.

I retreated into the yard. Standing on the cold bricks I heard the truck come up the alley, stop by stop, the whistle of the man dumping the cans telling the driver to move on, the muffled thuds of plastic cans, the grind of the crusher making room for another load—

I stood, nails in the palms of my hands, as they took Mrs. Rusling's trash, laughing, low-voiced as they worked. Even for garbage men, it was going to be a beautiful morning. Besides, they must almost be done. It would be full daylight soon.

The truck moved on.

I drove my nails into my palms, willing myself not to run after them, plead for them to sort through the trash—

One bird kept singing the same six or seven notes over and over. The leaves all rustled together as the air moved. I smelled the fresher wind from the hills that smelled of earth and rock and green, growing things. I was alone in a fine bright dawn.

The truck was gone.

Shalalire was gone, too.

East, over the rooftops, the sun was rising, gilding the blossoming clouds drifting west in the moving air. I went back up the cold brick walk, alone, unobserved, not even crying, just very, very tired, as if I hadn't slept at all. I leaned my face against the screen door, feeling the mesh pimple my forehead.

Somewhere off in the hills a fox barked, and barked again.

I lifted my head and listened, opened the screen door mechanically, let it close slowly behind me, careful not to wake the sleepers. The kitchen, smelling of clementines and dust, was dusky and dim. I leaned against the counter, not seeing anything.

Somewhere my great, shaggy stag lifted his forest-crowned head, heard the drumming feet and hooves of the hunt, and made his first stride—

Start with a good map, I thought. *Lay everything out.* I'd need drawing paper, India ink. This one would be completely mine, no silly games, no silly names, no compromises.

I picked up an orange from the counter, bounced it in my hand, began to peel it. Make it a quest for a golden—apple. Lots of good symbolism there. I bit into the first section I freed, felt the juice spurt in my mouth. I grinned and wiped juice from my chin with the back of my hand.

I must be sure to mention the Wild Hunt. In passing, of course. Just in passing. For Joanna.

It was a very good orange.

The Woman
Who Knew Better

M arilee banged the side of the old stove's firebox with
a stick of kindling to break up the ashes, then shook
the grate back and forth until the uncovered bed of
coals glowed red and even. She held a hand in the oven as
her lips moved in silent counting, then whipped it out, and
slammed the door to, hand muffled by the edge of her apron.

It'd be just about right by the time she needed it.

She reached up to the second dresser shelf, and took
down the biggest mixing bowl, the one that looked as if its
rim had been dipped in thick buttermilk that had run, here
and there, onto its sky blue belly.

Old Elijah Krober that was Dulcy's father—a good potter
with a bad tongue in his head—had made it more than thirty
years ago, before his kiln had burned to the ground and he
and all his family had been killed. But the bowl was just as
good as the day it was made. Better, maybe, for all its years
of knowing batters and biscuits.

Marilee filled the sifter from the flour bin and brought it
to the table, one hand under to save the floor. She shook
four heaping handfuls into the bowl, then paused to tuck a
loose strand of hair back into her tight, gray bun.

Then she was out the open door, across the well-swept
yard, down among the pine trees of Dulcy's grove, going to
the spring. There the butter crock sat nestled in the pebbled
bottom, half hidden by the ripples. For convenience's sake
the stoneware jar was secured by a string looped on an iron
peg driven deep in the kneeling stone. Marilee knelt and
pulled it out, automatically testing the water-logged cord with

a jerk between both hands. Still sound.

One hand on cold pottery, she stayed a moment to look at the pattern of branches across the sky, to listen to the sound of water spilling over into the patch of ferns downhill. Then her old knees protested the rock's smooth hardness just as her young ones had, and she rose quickly to her feet. Marilee had been kneeling there at least twice a day for sixty years and more.

She unfastened the crock from the string, made a tidy coil, knelt again to hang it on the peg, dipped her forefinger and drew a curlicue on the dry stone. Protection. Her great grandmother had done the same. Maybe her twice great gran, too. Slocum's was an old farm, with a date carved knuckle-deep in its thick, rough mantle. When they'd got the money for clapboards and the cabin was pulled down, the ancient chimney was left standing, and the new house built around it. The old place's well-seasoned logs had filled the fireplace the next winter.

But Dulcy's pool had been in use long before any log cabin had been here. There were arrowheads among the stones on the bottom, little ones, not much bigger than Marilee's thumbnail, black and thin, fluted along the edges where some ancient hand had knapped them. And before the worked stones had fallen in there had always been pebbles dancing in the boil, their fortune-telling patterns ignored by whatever came to drink.

Marilee looked and sniffed the air as she crossed the yard toward the weathered clapboard with its whitewashed door. Cold weather was nearly here. Having been battered by two seasons' worth of weather, the trees that climbed the hillsides all around had gone dull olive and rusty brown.

Brighter than gold, the late sunlight gilded each leaf of the maple at the gate. Its ragged crown shivered all over, once, despite the quiet air, then went completely still under Marilee's critical eye.

She frowned.

Slipping out from among the maple leaves were scraps of white, furling and unfurling, which might have been errant butterflies from the cabbage patch, if Marilee had planted cabbages this year. They drifted toward the ground, blew across the yard to linger above the doors of the old root cellar, then slipped around the corner of the house and were gone.

Marilee sniffed again, quite differently. Uppity, they were.

Inside, she put the crock on the corner of the table and untied the loop that held the wooden lid down. Cool water pooled on the tabletop, was sopped up with a fast swipe of the oldest dishtowel. She scooped out a lump of butter, half the size of her fist, with a deft twist. It was almost the last—she'd have to walk to Lester's tomorrow and hope his cow was still in milk. Then the old pastry cutter thumped its way across the bowl and back, fast as the hand could move, a blur to any watching eye.

It'd be biscuits, not cornbread, tonight. Fried ham. Greens that had been slowly simmering all the long afternoon. The tomato preserves Mrs. Willis had brought in trade. Haw jelly.

Marilee took pride in setting a good table.

She rolled the biscuits out, cut them with a floured water glass, lifted them onto the black baking sheet with a spatula, moving faster now, with an eye on the sky out the window that had somehow changed from afternoon to evening when she wasn't looking.

Down to the spring with crock and bucket, back with the bucketful of water for the first washing up, scrubbing the table, rinsing the bowl, setting the iron kettle on the back of the stovetop to heat for the real washing, after.

Quick, with a flick of her wrists, she shook the red-checked tablecloth open in the air and settled it in place. Then the wooden fork and spoon. The wooden-handled knife. The water glass with a stenciled white and green design of orange blossoms. The napkin in its deal ring of four hands clasped together, the last of the set her old uncle had carved for herself and her three sisters.

Marilee surveyed it all and pursed her lips with satisfaction.

A rainbird fluttered, frantic, against the lower panes of the window, and she took off her apron, leaned through the open door to shoo it away. She squinted up at the darkening sky. The lavender clouds were big-bellied with threats. *Showers later*, she thought.

Above the maple a cloudlet making its way against the wind caught her eye and stopped, drifting off unconcernedly, almost invisible against its bigger brothers billowing high in the air, their immense heights stained peach and rose with sunset.

Marilee sniffed once more, folding her apron crosswise then longwise into a tight, smooth bundle and draping it over one shoulder. Uppity. But it was about time anyway—dark *was* coming on. Already the tree shadows stretched long arms across the yard and the sun was down behind the hills.

She went over to the wooden, slanting doors of the old root cellar, drew the oak peg from the rusty hasp, and used it to rap on the planks. "Sonnyboy? You can come out now. Your things have been looking for you." She swung the hasp back on one side and stuck the peg back into the staple on the other.

One panel rose slowly up, releasing the scent of fresh-turned earth and rotting leaves. Something darker than the cellar's darkness growled and scrabbled at the iron door fastenings.

Marilee pulled the apron off her shoulder and fanned herself with the folded bundle. "Mind, don't hurt yourself. Sometimes I wonder if you have good sense." She looked into the gloom. "Come on up, now. Supper's ready."

There was a great whuff of dank air, and Sonnyboy's shaggy head peered out from the safe darkness. He mewed at the fading purple of the clouds.

"It's *past* sunset," said Marilee firmly. "Showers or no,

your father'll be waiting by Crowther's farm at full dark."

Sonnyboy slobbered a little, and mounted another stair.

Marilee fanned herself a bit more and went on, "You'd think Japhet Crowther would have learned by now. I've lost count how many cows he's had pulled down." She eyed the massive, hesitating form. "He bought new hens last Tuesday. Tell your daddy to look for eggs—no use your trying to gather them."

The huge, taloned hands worked helplessly.

"Shame on you for being shamed," she said tartly. "You know how your father depends on you."

Wooden planks thudded, and dust pattered down. Sonnyboy rose out of the earth, step by step.

"It'll be nice after midnight," Marilee said, turning away to give him a moment's privacy while his eyes adapted. His eyes did tear so when he looked into the light. "This breeze'll blow the clouds right through."

Sonnyboy huffed, and smelled the rising wind. In the dusk he was an enormous blackness pestered by a swirl of tiny glowworms hard to make out even in the shadows beneath the trees.

Half-formed intentions, no doubt. Marilee knew better than to pay any mind. His daddy'd find work for his idle hands.

Thinking of Sonnyboy's father, she bowed her head in silent homage. Japhet Crowther was foolish not to pay his respects. Everyone hereabouts did, just like their families always had. It did no harm to be respectful.

The Old Powers could surely be touchy if you weren't. Only a fool would set himself up to go against them. Elijah Krober had been just such a one. Dulcy'd been the only one to escape when the kiln went.

Marilee remembered the girl, barefoot in her white night shift, standing right there under the maple, face dyed red by the light of a fire a good half-mile away. "He didn't mean it," she kept wailing. "He didn't!"

Hysterical, the sheriff from Bixby said, and the locals had muttered something like agreement. Someone hunted up an old blanket for the girl and someone else brought sweet tea in a cracked cup. The three county officers stood about, swag bellies hanging over their belts, fussing over Dulcy until the fire burned low. It was a drought year, and they'd only come to see that the hillside didn't go, and a wildfire start on its way toward Bixby.

The wind just eddied around and around in Krober's hollow, building a pillar of flame that you could see for miles. The blaze died before dawn, leaving nothing but the burned-out kiln, the fireplace, and a few scorched trees.

A miracle, the sheriff said, in this dry weather.

Yes, indeed, everyone murmured. And it *was*.

Sonnyboy shuffled his feet and lifted his head to the growing dark. The first star winked on, then a second. Marilee's mouth went prim. The Powers were mostly forbearing if a man was drunk, sick, scared, or ignorant. But Elijah—

None of them had been surprised when the girl was found in Slocum farm pool, her long hair floating like waterweed. "Seen too much," said some of the old folks. "Made her bargain," other withered voices said. Marilee sniffed. As if *they* knew anything. Dulcy'd read the patterns in the stones at the bottom of the spring.

They'd buried the girl right *there*, under the pines—the blanket, the cup, and the body in the same old shift she'd died in. Death was a high price for a young girl to pay for her daddy's mouth, but Elijah'd known better than to say what he had. Respect was all the Powers demanded.

A course, if you offered more—

They could be neighborly.

Marilee suddenly smiled into the darkness. Fresh eggs would taste mighty good, fried, with plenty of bacon. Sonnyboy liked bacon almost as much as he liked ham. Better, some days.

"Supper," she said briskly, and went ahead to slake the stove with ashes.

"Ahh," breathed her son, a hoarse wind deep in his chest.

Shussssh went the trees in Dulcy's grove.

One Summer Evening

S ummer was the cruelest season. As the decades passed, the often-thwarted hope that he might heal had faded into despair, almost indifference, but when the long golden days came they always reminded him of what he once was and renewed his pain.

He knit his long fingers together and sighed. The girl laughed at him whenever she caught him in this mood, and he had become skilled at concealing his disquietude from her, if not from the three cats that lounged before the fire kept burning day and night regardless of the weather. Wiser than any human, they fled to the jungle safety of the garden whenever he unclasped the dark book bound in scaly leather.

So far the girl, who he had chosen for her sunny personality—he had a horror of clever women—had been right not to take him seriously. The book was as useless as he himself and might have gone to start the kitchen fire on some winter morning, except of course that the stove used gas.

Left knee creaking, he got to his feet to pace. That he had been exhausted when he had placed himself here at the conclusion of his failed labors was no excuse. What had then seemed overwhelmingly desirable, an obscure life filled with simple routines and mundane pleasures, was now not even tolerable. *Grief is always a bad counselor*, he reminded himself.

The hoarse, mechanical wail of a distant siren marred the summer air, and he frowned. When he had bound himself, he had known it would take great expertise to reverse the process. A delicate balance of influences had to be reached before he, with the, metaphorically speaking, small lever that was all he had allowed himself to retain, could once again move worlds.

Not being a total fool, even when grieving, he had not meant to make it impossible to change his mind. He was, after all, human, or nearly so. Still, in the end, his craft had failed him, or perhaps, in the prime of his powers he had underestimated what the loss of them would mean to him.

Turning, he looked out the open French doors. A late-evening mist was forming over the river. The garden's trunks, twigs, and leaves were picked and edged with the fleeting aureate of sunset. The sounds of the works of modern men grew dull and distant. Yet another perfect moment for the testing spell. He smiled bitterly. There had been many such.

And nothing had happened. How often he had sat waiting, offended by the distant rumble of airplanes, until the cats returned home and the girl came in from the kitchen. Redolent of herbs, spices, plus her own warm musk, she would lean on the arm of his chair and charm him into a better mood with wiles older than any man's.

Still, he thought, *I will not let this opportunity pass. If nothing else, I would always wonder if this was the time.* Taking the book from the shelf, he sat down, unclasped it, and smoothed the page carefully. Yet another try before he turned the television on for the evening and poured the first of what would be one too many drinks, if the girl did not beguile him to some other occupation. Checkers, chess, or the eroticisms that revealed a little too plainly how long it had been since she was as naive as she liked to pretend.

I cannot grudge her little deceit, he thought. *How long has it been since I was an innocent? Never, perhaps, given my parentage and childhood. She does well by me, and old men must make compromises young ones would never admit. Glory is the stuff of youth, as diplomacy is of age.*

Focusing his mind, he reread the instructions he had penned so long ago. He trusted that older self as he did not trust his present one. Besides, magicking from memory without dire need was ostentatious. He had always preferred discretion when discretion would serve as well or better than showy workings.

Somewhere beyond the garden wall a car hooted urgently and was answered by an angry chorus of horns. He winced, then spread his hands and spoke, feeling his tongue twist and curl reluctantly around syllables never meant for any human mouth. As he spoke, the hide on the book shuddered against his thighs, as if it were a living thing, stirring in deep sleep.

Or perhaps his legs had quivered with the obscure tensions of age. The signs were on him. He had not much longer, and he had never believed in anything other than the four powers, earth, air, fire, and water. They had served him, and he, they. Having gone beyond the appearance to the reality, he tried to be—

Begin, said a voice in his mind and he did. Spell muttered and sighed into the summer twilight, he leaned back, eyes closed. The scrabble of a cat's claws on the hearth bricks woke him from his doze. The gray tabby had caught a mouse or, the ancient exile leaned forward in his chair, perhaps it was a bat.

Eyes narrowing suddenly, he held out a hand and compelled the animal to him with a skill long disused. Then he prodded the small carcass with a long forefinger before giving it back to its rightful owner.

Head high to keep the wings from dragging, the offended tabby carried the tiny dragon off to its private lair under the blackberry brambles. The other two cats drew as near as they dared, and crouched, tails lashing, hissing. In the silence, you could hear the plop and ripple of the river.

Hands palm up, open, on the book in his lap, he felt power begin to fill the hollow in his soul. A swirl of vapor formed above the garden's beech trees. Looking up from its fabulous feast, the gray tabby yowled. Fat raindrops splattered the paving, wept down the glass of the open French doors. The cats bolted into the house as the first stroke of lightening slashed the air. Thunder walked the sky.

Merlin laughed.

The End

These Works Published In

Peacock Dancer
Warrior, Wisewoman 2, Norilana Books, 2009

Greenwife
Tomorrow SF, v1.7, Spring, 1997

Blood Moon
Sword and Sorceress XXIII, Norilana Books, 2008

The Decisive Princess
Sword and Sorceress XXII, Norilana Books, 2007

The End of the Dream Time
Whitley Strieber's Aliens, Simon & Schuster (Pocket Books),
1999

The Ragged Man
Odyssey, Third Wave Publications, 1994

The Hungry Season
The Hunting of the Monster Bear, Copper Penny Press, October
2007

Heaven Shed Tears
Warrior, Wisewoman , Norilana Books, 2008

Summer-Witch
Tomorrow SF, v13.8, Summer, 1997

Terra Incognita
Keene Science Fiction, December, 1996

The Woman Who Knew Better
TransVersions, whole number three, 1995

One Summer Evening
Weird Tales, whole number 316, 1999